Arte Público Press
Houston, Texas
1996

This volume is made possible through grants from the National Endowment for the Arts (a federal agency), the Andrew W. Mellon Foundation and the Lila Wallace-Reader's Digest Fund.

Recovering the past, creating the future

Arte Público Press
University of Houston
Houston, Texas 77204-2090

Cover illustration and design by James F. Brisson

Yglesias, Jose
The guns in the closet / by Jose Yglesias.
p. cm.
Contents: The guns in the closet — In the Bronx — The American sickness — Ordinary things — The place I was born — The girls on the block — Celia's family — The gardens of Long Island — What hurts — An idea for a story.
ISBN 1-55885-182-8 (cloth: alk. paper)
ISBN 1-55885-162-3 (pbk: alk. paper)
1. Minorities—United States—Fiction. 2. Ethnic groups—United States—Fiction. 3. United States—Social life and customs—20th century—Fiction. I. Title.
PS3575.G5G86 1996
813'.54—dc20 96-13275
CIP

The paper used in this publication meets the requirements of the American National Standard for Permanence of Paper for Printed Library Materials Z39.48-1984.∞

For Anita and Alfred Geto, old friends.

Contents

The Guns in the Closet 9

In the Bronx 35

The American Sickness 58

Ordinary Things 77

The Place I Was Born 87

The Girls on the Block 96

Celia's Family 115

The Gardens of Long Island 129

What Hurts 146

An Idea for a Story 160

The Guns in the Closet

The Guns in the Closet

Until now, Tony believed he had been liberated by his Venezuelan grandfather's name—freed to be the special person that for years he unthinkingly felt himself to be. Ybarra. "Basque, you know," he would say when the subject came up. He was an editor in a New York publishing house, and author of an occasional essay, and it was understood, especially by European editors visiting his office, that his name set him apart from—well, whatever American foolishness or provinciality or philistinism infected the scene at the moment. He was aware that there was more than a trace of snobbery in this; aware, too, of the defensive residue, for he never forgot the discrimination that his name had subjected him to—mild, he admitted—during his adolescence in New York public schools and even at Harvard, though never in publishing, he liked to believe. Motel desk clerks in New England and the Midwest still took a second look at him when they noticed the name on the charge card, and allowed his appearance and his speech to convince them that he was all right. Those tiny encounters when he stood for inspection kept him, he thought, open to the world of the ghettos—the blacks, Puerto Ricans, and Chicanos—and it pleased him that his son, Bill, who he had made sure learned Spanish fluently, should have lately come alive to the name. It amused him when Bill referred to himself in company—so as not, perhaps, to be challenged by his parents—as a Third World person. Today, Tony was uneasy.

Bill had come down from the apartment near Columbia University that he shared with other students—like him, activists who had been suspended after the campus strike—to have Sunday brunch at home. A surprise, for these were not family brunches, and Tony knew that Bill could no longer bear the two or three writers and editors, all West Side liberal neighbors, who would be there. "It's the Third World that's important, not the American moral conscience!" he had yelled one Sunday three months earlier. "Up the NFL!" And he had not been back since. Today, Bill sat out the two pitchers of Bloody Marys, the quiche, the fruit salad, the French loaves and cheeses from Zabar's, and tension grew between him and Tony as suppressed as Bill's opinions were today.

Tony thought about his old friend, Clifford, who would have been here if he were not in Algiers on a writing assignment. "Dear chaps, you're luckier with Bill than others are with their children," he'd said the last time Tony and his wife, Gale, had discussed Bill with him. "*They* deal with their kids as if they were a declining power negotiating with a newly emerged nation. The new diplomacy, right?"

Right. Tony saw that Gale had caught him studying Bill, and he smiled thinly, as if to say *Don't ask me*. And Bill, of course, intercepted all this and, unseen by the guests, winked at his parents, as if he in turn were replying *I'm here, that's all*. But later, when the others had left, he offered to go down with his father to walk the dog, and Gale explained triumphantly, "Aha!" Bill laughed helplessly as in the days when he was a boy and they had uncovered one of his ruses.

"Shall I take money with me?" Tony asked as if asking an audience.

"No money," Gale said.

Bill shook his head and threw up his arms. A routine family charade, and Tony decided that his anxiety was baseless. But when Bill was saying good-bye, Gale took the boy's head between her hands, as she had begun to do during the strike at Columbia, and kissed him. Trouble, Tony thought; she always knows.

Going down in the elevator, both quiet in the presence of other tenants, Tony noticed that Bill wore a J. Press jacket he had not seen in a long time. No army fatigue jacket. His hair was almost short, his pants were not jeans, his shoes were not work boots, and there were no Panther buttons on his chest. He seemed to have abandoned the new lifestyle, and it surprised Tony that his son's appearance did not please him; he looked ordinary.

Ordinary? Then he must not be a Weatherman. Thinking about Bill afflicted Tony with non sequiturs. "Bill, you don't have money to keep your apartment, do you?" he said. "You're not there anymore. We haven't been able to reach you for two weeks."

Bill shook his head. "No," he said. "but I don't want to be up there anymore."

So he was downtown. "Are you in a commune?"

Bill pulled the dog toward Riverside Drive. "Too many people on Broadway," he explained, and crossed the drive to the park. When Tony caught up with him, he was bending down to unleash the dog and let him run.

"Well, are you in a commune?" Tony asked, and smiled to appear casual.

From his bent position, Bill looked up and smiled a mocking smile; he shook his head. Tony was not reassured—not even when Bill straightened, threw out his arms, and took a deep breath, as if that was what he had come out for. Bill began to jog down the path to the esplanade and motioned his father on. "Good for you! he called, and again he went through the motions of inhaling and exhaling with vigor.

When Tony got to him, he said, "Listen, Dad, I'd like to bring some stuff down tonight from my place. For you to keep for me. Just for a couple of days."

There were people brushing by. "Sure," Tony said, thinking it was books or clothes. "We're not going out. Anyway, you have a key." Bill looked at him so seriously that Tony stopped, suspicious again. "What stuff?"

Bill turned his head away. They were alone on the path now. "Guns," he said quietly.

Later, Tony wished he could have seen his son's face when he said that, but only the back of his neck was in view. There were wet leaves on the ground, and everything was still. Then a burst of laughter from a group of young people who appeared in the path on their way out of the park. They crowded Tony to one side and gave him time to think. I must not show my fear, he thought, especially my fear for him. But the questions burst out of him like exclamations. "They're not yours, are they? Whose are they?"

"No questions like that," Bill said. In a moment, he added, "Of course, they don't belong to *me*."

"I see," Tony said, subdued. They had come onto the esplanade and there were people everywhere, walking their dogs, sitting on the benches, or simply strolling. Tony did not know whether it was their presence that forced him to speak causally, that created a new equality between him and Bill, or the boundaries that Bill had set up. I do not own this part of him, he thought; I can say yes or no, but that is all. He had liked being a father and it shamed him now that he was elated, as he walked alongside him, to find that Bill had his own mysterious corners, his own densities.

Finally, he said, "I shall have to talk to Gale first. It's her decision, too." He had never, with Bill, called Gale anything but "your mother," and he knew he was being mean in his new equality. Both to Bill and to his wife. Bill could walk away from their lives—perhaps even should—but parentage cannot be removed. He reached out and touched Bill's shoulder.

"O.K.," Bill said. "You tell me when I phone you later."

But he had come to me—*me*—and in the wind that blew from the river, Tony's eyes teared. "You said they were at your place," he said. "Is that uptown?"

Bill nodded.

"And your friends living there—do they know?"

Bill exhaled and began his explanations. "They were away last weekend and the FBI broke in. The kids next door told them about it. The agents went through their apartment to get to the fire escape—it's kind of hard to get into ours with the locks I have on the door—and the kids came home while the agents were there. The super had let the two of them in, but the kids told them to get out. So the pieces have to be removed right away. They were just lying under the bed in duffel bags—they must have seen them. My friends have been trying to get to me all week."

"And the apartment is in your name!"

Bill did not answer.

"You can bring them," Tony said. "It will be all right with your mother, I'm sure."

"O.K.," Bill said. "I have to go now." He handed his father the leash. "I'll call you tonight." The dog followed him, and he turned back after a few paces. "Listen, when I call I'll ask if I can sleep over and tell you how soon I'll be there. You be down on the street when I arrive."

"All right," Tony said, and the sound of his voice was so strange to him that he leaned down to hold the dog to hide his sensation. Bill's legs did not move away, so Tony looked up and saw him bring a hand up to his waist and make it into a fist quickly, casually.

"All power to the people," Bill said in a conversational voice. Then he smiled, in order, as they said in their family, to take the curse off it. "See you."

Alone, Tony felt cool and lightheaded. He wanted to run and did, and the dog ran after him. Nothing unusual—the kind of sprint that men walking dogs in the park will often break into. During the war, he had reacted this way when, as pilot on a scout observation plane, he climbed to the catwalk and into his plane to be catapulted from the ship: his hands checked the canopy, the stick between his legs—all concentration while his emotions unreeled without control and unrelated images flitted in and out of his mind. He knew only that he was being observed and that he must be true to some unconfessed vision of himself.

He walked back to the apartment slowly. How to tell Gale. Dinner guests would have to be put off. Last summer, the caretaker of the Maine estate they rented had asked him what kind of name his was, and when he replied that it was Spanish—no use saying Basque—the old man had said, "Spanish! Now, there's nothing wrong with that, is there?" The guns must go in the closet in his study—that was one place their thirteen-year-old daughter, who now should be back from her friend's apartment, never looked.

In the elevator, he thought, but if *they* didn't come back to the apartment with warrants, then they must have a reason to wait. Do they hope to catch Bill? Do they have a watch on the place, and if Bill walks out in a few hours with... He could not say this to Gale. She was lying on the living room couch with the Sunday Times, and he got a pad and pen and sat next to her and wrote out the conversation—the gist of it—he had had with Bill.

Gale smiled when he handed it to her, but when she had read it she sat up. "But—" she began. Behind her came the wail of a Beatles record from their daughter's room.

Tony put a finger to his lips. "Not here," he said.

The color went out of her face. "I've got to go out for a cup of coffee," she said. "Right now!"

They walked up and down Broadway and sat in a coffee shop and talked. She wanted to be angry at someone. "Couldn't you have brought him back to the apartment?" she said.

Tony felt like putting his head in his hands. "I didn't think..."

She waved a hand defeatedly, in understanding. "And there's no way of getting in touch with him?"

By the time they returned to the apartment, the exhilaration he had first felt was gone. They were no sooner inside than Gale had to take up the pad and write on it a warning about their daughter: *She must now know unless it is absolutely necessary*. He nodded, noticing the misspelling. And the cleaning woman who came three times a week, she wrote. She must be kept out of his study. He nodded again and took the sheet from the pad and went into the small bath off the study and tore it into small pieces and flushed them down the toilet. Thank God, Gale had not thought of the danger to Bill when he removed the guns from the apartment uptown.

Tony sat in the study and knew that Gale was restlessly tidying the apartment. Later, he heard her on the phone calling off the evening's appointment, arguing with their daughter to keep her from having friends in. Then silence. He could not read or write. He kept visualizing the walk-up near Columbia, which he had visited only three or four times. So many of the tenants were young people moving in and out that surely duffel bags would attract no attention. He thought of the solution: a decoy. Someone must first leave with the duffel bags that had been under the bed, but with something else in them. Of course. He got up from his chair to tell Gale. No. It was Bill he should get to. Run up to the apartment? Ten minutes by taxi. Gale wouldn't notice.

He had taken his jacket out of the hall closet when he realized that he dare not be seen up there today. Which of Bill's friends could he call? Which of them had gone this far with him in his politics? He did not know. He told Gale, who was lying on the couch again, that he was going down for cigarettes. She looked blank, then questioning, and Tony smiled and shook his head. From a street booth, he called a friend of Bill's who had been with him in the Columbia strike. The operator came on and asked what number he was calling. He told her—safe enough in a public booth, he thought. In a moment, she came back on to say the number had been disconnected. When he got back to the apartment, Gale did not look up from the couch. As he put his jacket back in the closet, he saw that she would not look up. She had thought of the danger.

He went to his study and tried not to think. There was a manuscript in his briefcase that one of the young editors liked. Another book on Vietnam. They already had one for the winter list. It was foolish not to talk aloud to Gale in the apartment. He could not believe the FBI had time to listen to his phone, to the hours of his daughter's, his wife's, and his own conversations, just because of Bill. He remembered a manuscript on surveillance that his house had turned down. To cover the whole apartment, the sound would have to be transmitted to a nearby station no more than two or three blocks away, to be either recorded or monitored. Thank God, he was not a paranoid left-winger.

Yet when the phone rang at eleven forty-five and he heard Bill say, "Dad?" he gave way to the fear that had made him write on the pad. He had to clear his throat before he could answer.

"Listen, Dad, I'm in the neighborhood." His voice was easy—he was a good actor. "I'm at a party and I don't want to go all the way downtown when I leave, so I'm going to do you and Mom the honor of staying with you overnight. O.K.?"

"O.K.," he said, and knew he was not playing his part well. He tried to ask the question. "Bill..."

"I'll be there in an hour," Bill said with that touch of highhanded misuse of parents that had once been genuinely his. "Thanks," he added, out of character.

"Bill..." Tony began again and then did not risk it.

After a pause Bill said, "See you then," and hung up.

The next hour would tell. Tony went to the bedroom where Gale was watching a talk show and said with the casualness he had not managed on the phone that Bill was coming by in an hour to spend the night. She looked at him with the kind of reproach that women transmit with a glance when they think their men ware acting like boys. He shrugged, went to the kitchen, heated some coffee, and drank it in his study. Once *this* was over, he told himself, he would make Bill have a long talk with him. There had been no battles during his adolescence—none of the rows that are usual with fathers and sons—and he did not want Bill's activities now, whatever they were, to be surrogates for them. He had been proud when Bill so suddenly, at Columbia, had become political; he had alerted everyone at the office when Bill was scheduled to appear on a program last year of the show Gale was now watching. He had not used parental concern as an excuse for trying to keep him at school or to deflect him—not even when, after Dean Rusk had spoken at the new Hilton, Bill came home battered from a fight with the cops on Sixth Avenue.

Ten minutes before the hour was up, Tony went downstairs. Between midnight and one, the doorman was always in the basement helping the janitor wheel the garbage cans onto the street by the side entrance. A police car was parked at the corner, its lights on; one cop stood at the back entrance of the bakery two doors down, waiting for the pastry they cadged each night, and the other was at the all-night diner for coffee. Tony lit a cigarette and stood at the door of the building as if he had come out for a breath of air. There were still many people on Broadway, but fewer, and the prostitutes were more visible. The cops went back to their car to drink the coffee and eat the Danish. He raised a hand in greeting when one looked his way, and both of them grinned. Nothing suspicious about me, he thought; I'm a respectable, middle-aged West Sider.

The cops pulled out as soon as they were finished, having lit cigarettes and set their faces into the withdrawn, contemptuous expressions that signified they were back on the job. A Volks station wagon turned into the street, paused, and then parked where the patrol car had been. Bill sat next to the driver; the friend Tony had tried to call earlier was behind the wheel. Tony walked over as Bill got out; his friend stayed inside and did not turn off the engine.

"Everything all right?" Tony asked.

"Great!" Bill said. He walked to the back of the car, opened the window, and beckoned with his head. There were two long leather cases lying in the car; they looked handsome and rich. "Golf clubs," Bill said, and picked up one and handed it to Tony. He took the other, fitted an arm through its strap, and carried it over one shoulder. With his free hand he waved to his friend, and the car drove off.

"Thank God, you didn't bring them in the duffel bags," Tony said, almost gaily. "I wanted to call and tell you that you should first have left the house with the duffel bags and then…"

"That's what we did," he said. "Sent a decoy out first."

Tony put his arm through the strap of the second case and walked alongside Bill to the entrance of the apartment building. We are the perfect picture of the middle-class father and son, he thought. I would say, seeing the two of us, that we belong to a country club in Westchester, play tennis from spring to late fall, swim, golf, of course, and keep a boat at the Seventy-ninth Street Basin. During the winter, we get together at the Athletic Club for handball, followed by a short swim in the heated pool. The son dashes out immediately after, but the father gets a rubdown and later joins two or three others his age for lunch upstairs by the wide, tall windows looking down on Central Park. Ah, yes. His Venezuelan grandfather's name and his childhood in the Spanish section of Chelsea would keep him always on a circular stage slowly revolving to the view: you never cease to act the role that the eyes of others create.

Tony said, "You're going to find your mother very upset."

"About this?" Bill said. "I'll talk to her."

"Well, not inside," Tony advised. "We've been careful to say nothing that we wouldn't want overheard."

Bill looked down, but Tony saw he was amused. "Well, Dad, it's not very likely." he said in the lobby. "Their tapping equipment must be overtaxed these days. Too many groups into heavy stuff, you know." And in the elevator he explained, in such detail that it alarmed Tony that he should know the subject so well, how you can detect with the use of an FM radio whether there is a bug in the apartment.

"We have to talk about you," Tony said. "I don't know what *you* are into, and it worries me."

"Sure, O.K.," Bill said. They were on their floor, about to turn to the door of their apartment. "Look, you know I'm grateful to you that I learned Spanish and something about the culture. I got you to thank for that." He stopped, and Tony thought there must be many things Bill did not thank him for. "But I'm a Third World person, you know, and that's how I'm going to live."

Gale was not at the front of the apartment. Tony led Bill through the dining room and kitchen to the study. They leaned the cases against the back wall of the closet, and when they closed the door on them Bill said, "It'll only be for a couple of days. We'll let you know when."

"Remember, I stay home Tuesdays to read manuscripts," Tony said.

"O.K.," Bill said, nodding, and on the way to the living room turned and added, "It won't be me."

Gale was standing in the living room in her robe. She held one hand up in a fist and shook it at Bill in pretended anger. He laughed. Well, for Christ's sake, Tony thought.

She asked, "Can I make you something to eat?"

"No time, Mom," Bill said. "I've got to go."

"But you said—" Tony began.

Gale completed it: "You were staying overnight!"

Bill's expression reminded them of his old joke that his parents talked like an orchestra. "I can't. My friend is waiting for me."

"But he drove away," Tony said.

"I saw him from my window," Gale added.

"He's two blocks farther down, waiting." Bill walked over to his mother to say good-bye. "I'll be in touch."

Tony watched her hug him but could not hear what she whispered in his ear. When she let him go, she was pale and ready to cry. Tony said, "I'm coming down with you."

In the hall, he tried to tell Bill some of the things he had thought that day. They came out badly. "I have to tell you that I don't agree with what you're doing.

They're the wrong tactics. They won't work here. You don't know what real Americans are. You'll bring down the most—"

"Christ, Dad, you're not on the Susskind program." That special hardness was in his voice; Tony did not know where he got it. "You know all the arguments as well as I do. Remember the time you came off his talk show and said there's just no way to make radical change palatable to liberals like that?"

"You're not going to compare me to him!"

"Not unless you force me," Bill said, and stopped because people had got on the elevator.

In the lobby, Tony let them go ahead. He said quietly, as if making a new start, "I'm worried about what's going to happen to you."

"Don't worry, I'm learning karate," Bill said seriously. "No pig is going to run me down and twist my arm behind my back. From now on we're doing the Bogarting. Twice a week I go to Connecticut to the rifle range and practice shooting." He laughed. "I need a lot of practice."

"What's that for!"

"I've got a very simple test for radicals," Bill said. "When I read about some radical movement, I ask, did they arm themselves, did they pick up the gun? If they didn't, they aren't serious."

On Broadway, Tony flinched when he saw a middle-aged writer coming toward them with his young wife—his third. They had the giggly look of people who have been turning on. And an after-the-party boredom with one another. Tony introduced them to Bill, and the writer made an effort to focus on him. "Pretty quiet at Columbia this year," he said. "Anything happening?"

"I wouldn't know," Bill said.

Quickly, Tony asked the writer how the new novel was doing. He began to talk about the reviews. Tony saw Bill edge away, and the writer tried to hold him by saying, "Say, you ought to take a look at it. It's a revolutionary book."

"We have to go," Tony said. "I'll call you tomorrow."

Bill was down the block and the writer called, "Read the book, kid. It'll blow your mind!"

Tony was breathless with the need to say something to his son that would somehow get to—what? He didn't know; he simply exhaled when he reached his side.

Bill shook his head. "Don't worry," he said, as if he understood. The Volks station wagon was at the corner waiting, and Bill paused. "You know, I've been down to Fourteenth Street several times, eating at the Spanish restaurants and sitting at the bars. A couple of old Republicans like Fidel, but none speak well about the Puerto Ricans." He shook his head again.

"Well..."

"You say your grandfather was an anarchist—right?" Bill asked. "Did you talk to him much? I got to talk to you about him. Sometime. O.K.?"

"Yes, yes," Tony said. He wondered what that old man—wearing a beret while he fixed the windows and doors in the worn-out apartment and built cages for the pigeons on the roof—had thought of him and his books.

When he got back home, he found Gale lying in bed reading. He felt sure she had been to the closet in his study. She looked up when he took out his robe and began to undress. "I don't want to talk about it until they're gone," she said. "And that had better be soon or I shall go out of my mind." He didn't answer, and after a moment she asked, "When is that going to be?"

"Two days," he said, but he did not really know. He lay next to her, his arms folded over his chest, and went over everything Bill had said. He could not quite remember what was to happen. Someone would get in touch with him. There were the facts of Bill's day-to-day life to piece together. And all that rhetoric. He was going to live like a Third World person. What the hell did that mean? This is the real generation gap, he thought—you can't grab hold of these kids; they sum up your life and their own in a phrase and leave you gasping. They wrench you out of the dense element that is your daily life and there you are—on the shore, on the shore, on the shore.

At breakfast next morning, Gale announced that she was going to do volunteer work at the public school all week. Penance for sending their own to private schools, but also this week, he suspected, to be out of the way.

Tony went to the office late. There had been no call at the apartment, and there was no call here, either. He returned early with three manuscripts to read the next day. Again, no call. Gale was not home and he took the dog and headed for the Drive, as if that would help him recall his talk with Bill. He let the dog loose and stood at the parapet at the esplanade and smoked and stared at the river.

A short, dark man who looked to Tony like a typical Puerto Rican came over with an unlit cigarette, asking for a light. Tony handed him his cigarette and he held it delicately and took a light from it. He looked Tony directly in the eye when he thanked him. He did not walk away but turned to study the river, too, and it was then Tony realized that the man had spoken to him in Spanish. "If you are home tomorrow morning," he said now, still in Spanish, "someone will come to pick up the packages you have been so kind to hold for us."

Tony smiled in a kind of reflex and found that he could not turn on his fake smile. He thought, this is a trap; I must get away. Instead, he replied in Spanish, "For us?"

"Your son did not tell you whose they are?" He had the sweet accent of Puerto Ricans.

Tony shook his head.

The man said, "MIRA. Have you heard of us?"

Tony nodded. The bombings in the Bronx. An underground terrorist group operating in New York. A bad manuscript called "Colonies in the Mother Country" had mentioned them. Crazily, he wondered if he had been right to reject it.

The man seemed to watch all this going on in his head, and as if to help him added, "We are madmen."

"Talk to me," Tony said, and pointed to a bench. "What about my son?"

"Your son?" The man waited for him to sit first, bowing a little and standing to one side. "But you must know better than we do—if he trusted you with packages. What can I tell you?"

"We are very worried about his activities," Tony replied. "I do not want you to divulge anything that is confidential, but if you can tell me something..."

"Oh, there do not have to be any mysteries between us," the man said, and looked around at a man going by with a dog. He waited until he had passed. "Your son is very much of an Hispano. He is closer in feeling to us, he says, than to any of the others."

"Others?"

"The other revolutionary groups," he explained. "American ones. We are all in touch. He is a liaison man with us. There are certain things that a Puerto Rican cannot do. It looks funny for us to be in certain places or buy certain things. Too conspicuous. You understand?"

Tony nodded and looked at the river, trying to place Bill in all this. His dog came back to the bench and the man leaned down and patted him. "What a friendly little dog he is," he said. "My younger brother was killed in the independence uprising after the war. Just one of the many killed in Puerto Rican towns all over the island... One of our problems is getting guns to comrades on the island," he said inconsequentially, talking as if this might help Tony. "What better proof that we are an oppressed colony than the fact that guns, which are so easy to come by in these states, are almost impossible for Puerto Ricans to obtain."

"The laws are not the same?" Tony said.

"Jesus Christ himself could not qualify to own a gun there."

Tony took out a pack of cigarettes and offered it. The Puerto Rican accepted with the grace that only a Latin seems able to put into such a gesture. “I admired your article on the Latin-American revolutionaries very much,” he said, and Tony was startled—could this man have read the quarterly in which he had published two essays in the last five years? “The one on their situation after the death of Che. I had not known that wonderful saying of Marti’s: ‘El arbol que mas crece es el que tiene un muerto por debajo.’” (“The tree that grows tallest has a dead man buried beneath it.”)

“That is what I fear,” Tony said.

The man squinted and then struck himself on the forehead. “What a fool I am! You ask me about your son. You are worried like a good father, and all I talk about is dying and killing. Forgive me, compañero.” They were quiet a moment. The Puerto Rican looked at his cigarette and flicked the ash off it carefully. “It is true that for us it is especially necessary to think about the possibility of death, to get used to it even. But that is not what interests us—that does not interest us one bit.”

“Forgive me if I tell you that I do not think you have a chance,” Tony said.

“That, too, does not interest us,” the Puerto Rican replied very gently, in a tone that seemed solely concerned with Tony’s feelings.

Tony got up and, because he was suddenly ashamed at the abruptness with which he was ending their talk, extended his hand.

The man took it in both of his. “I know what it is you are too polite to say,” he said. “That your son is not a Puerto Rican. But do you not find that wonderful? Is not that the best guarantee that we will win this time?

Look, those Young Lords in the barrio want to free Puerto Rico, too, but almost none of them can really speak Spanish. Some of the older nationalists cannot believe in them, but I say it is what is here"—he stopped to place a hand on his own heart—"that matters."

"I wish you success," Tony said.

The man nodded slowly, solemnly. Then he smiled. "Perhaps we shall see one another again. If you go to the island to write one of your studies, there are people we would like you to meet. See what Yankees we have become—we know the value of publicity now, even if only among the professors who read the magazines where you publish." He laughed and added, "At ten tomorrow morning then, a girl will ask you one more favor—to help her take the packages to her car."

It was Gale's custom to look at him carefully when she greeted him—her way of asking for news—but today she began a story about a Taiwanese child at school, so pointedly, Tony felt, that it was a rebuff. When she stopped, he said, "Tomorrow."

She stepped over to him and pecked him on the cheek. "How do you know?" she whispered.

He lied. "Bill called."

The phone rang, and Gale picked it up. "Cliff!" she exclaimed.

"Tell him to come over," Tony called. Back from Algiers, thank God—the one person he could talk to about all this.

"He heard you," Gale said, "but he hasn't unpacked."

Tony insisted, as eager as when they had been undergraduates, "Tell him to come over and we'll open cans for dinner—I want to discuss business."

Clifford had spent a month in Algiers talking to Eldridge Cleaver. The last time they had spent an old-fashioned evening together, Tony had come up with the idea of the trip, and he did want to know if Clifford was going to get a book out of it. He wanted to talk about simultaneous hardcover and paperback publication, but it was really the chance to spend the evening with something in mind other than the guns in the closet that attracted him. And the possibility that Clifford could help with Bill.

Clifford had got a bottle of Cuban añejo through customs and he held it out in greeting. "Limes and Seven-Up!" he called. "I feel like my comic-strip name—Clifford Moon!"

Gale said, "You don't look it!"

He was wearing a Pierre Cardin vest suit and a flowered silk shirt with wide sleeves. In the month he had been away his sideburns had grown long and bushy; his mustache curved over the corners of his lips. He stretched out on a chair and showed his Moroccan slippers—sheepskin with embroidery.

"In Algiers, everyone is stoned all the time," Clifford said, beginning on his first Mojito—a Cuban drink he had brought back from trips made to cover the Cuban revolution. "You really should have fresh mint for this, but it'll do. They just don't know what the joys of drinking are in Algiers. I think I shall have to take a stand against hash, pot, grass—what inelegant names! It turns everyone into lobotomized types."

"Never mind all that," Tony said. "Have you got a book?"

"Dear chaps, I've scarcely been allowed to turn the experience over in my mind," he replied, and he let his arms droop down the sides of his chair. "I haven't even called my agent."

Tony waved a hand. "Oh, your agent—we've already discussed it."

"Did he say there won't be any minimum royalty on the paperback?" Clifford asked, sitting forward.

"Well..."

"I want more than the five per cent for my share," Clifford said. He laughed. "I'm getting myself a fur coat this winter."

"Well!" Tony said, and he didn't know if it was envy that made him decide then that he could not discuss Bill.

Gale said, "Let's drive down to Washington together for the Kent State demonstration. Or do you have to work?"

"Yes, no—yes!" Clifford said. "Dear me, I mean yes. There'll be beautiful, young people there from all over the country. They're bound to get stoned and disrobe—like Woodstock. And I can work that into the book." He picked up his drink from the floor and looked slyly at Tony over the rim of his glass. "How the revolution sells nowadays. Though I don't know to whom. The young don't read. I daresay it's the anxious middle-aged who want to know what their children are doing. In the fifties they would've gone to their analysts. This is better for us." He looked sly again. "Right, chaps?"

Promptly at ten the next morning, the downstairs buzzer sounded. Alone in the apartment, Tony opened the door, and a few minutes later watched the girl walk from the elevator toward him. She wore a maxi raincoat unbuttoned over a mini skirt. Her legs were stunning. "Is everything all right?" he asked.

"Oh, hi!" she said, delighted. "I'm parked just across from you."

He had thought that if she was alone he would have to make two trips with the cases, but she touched her right biceps and said, "Muscles," and took one of them. Tony watched the doorman study her legs when he held the door open for them. Damn. The writer whose new novel was just out was on the sidewalk—alone this time.

"Hey!" the writer said. "You didn't call."

"Stay right there," Tony said, following the girl. "I'll be right back." She opened the trunk of a Mercedes Benz at the opposite curb, and while he placed his case in it, Tony was aware that the writer watched them.

She brushed her long hair back when she straightened, and said, "Thanks."

"O.K.?" Tony said, wondering if he should shake hands.

"A message from Bill—he won't be in touch for a while," she said with a smile.

"What!" he said.

"Your friend is waiting," she said, and turned away.

He hovered as she got in behind the wheel. "Tell him we want to see him, please," he said, and watched her smile in that nonwavering, idiotic way.

When he got back to the writer, they watched her drive off. Without looking at him, the writer said, "You play golf?"

"Me?" Tony asked. "Oh, no, just helping a neighbor."

"Wow!" he replied. "You got that in your building!"

When Tony walked into the apartment, it felt eerie, like the time they returned from the theater to find that someone had broken in. He went straight to the study and closed the door to the closet. He could not concentrate on the manuscripts he had brought home. He made a cup of coffee and tried to think of what Bill's message meant. He would not tell Gale. On the radio in the study, the news commentators said that the national revulsion against the Kent State killings was escalating. The third time he heard the same news on the hour break, he turned the radio off and remembered Bill's instructions about how to find a tapping bug. He flicked the radio on again and dialed to the low end of the band and slowly moved up. On the third try, he caught a faint beep. He held the dial there; it built in volume. With both hands he picked up the radio and moved in the direction of the wall phone. The beep became steadier and louder: the tap was there. With shaking hands Tony put the radio back on its shelf and turned it off. Something else to keep to himself.

Later in the week, he and Gale went to Washington with Clifford and walked among the young people on the green. He looked for Bill, letting Gale and Clifford sit through the speeches while he roamed. He came back exhausted, and when Gale said, "Aren't they beautiful?" he could only nod, because his eyes were full of tears and his throat was tight. He felt better for being there, but on the way home anxiety returned; and each time a bomb exploded that winter he fought back the desire to call the police and find out, before the *Times* got to the stands, who was involved. He went to all the demonstrations. They were dear to him. He looked at the young people, no longer searching for his son, who had never called, and said inwardly, over and over, without irony, accepting his country at last while he repeated Bill's name in Spanish—Guillermo Ybarra—*I commend my son, fellow Americans, to your care.*

In the Bronx

Clara had only to get up and say good night and Harris would follow. She had met him for the first time this evening—their hosts believed that a film editor like her and an assistant producer of a daytime television show should do well together—and they had outstayed all the dinner guests. It was one in the morning, there was no question he would offer to take her home, and she would say yes. Clara stood up and then the phone rang. "I must say good night, too," Harris said as their hostess disappeared into her bedroom. Again they exchanged smiles. "How about one last drink?" their host asked, and got no reply because the phone call was for Clara. Her daughter, Tina. Fourteen and no problem, she had told Harris that evening. Now she felt foolish, as if she had been discovered playacting, and then worried, because indeed Tina was no problem. She hurried to the phone in the bedroom, hearing her host call after her, "I'm sure it's nothing—Tina sounded fine."

"Tina?" she said into the mouthpiece.

"Listen, Mother, your cousin Estela called." Tina paused, and Clara knew she meant to calm her. Tina and her WASP father always behaved as if Latins need to be calmed. "From the Bronx."

"When did she call?"

"Just now." She paused again and Clara waited. "Listen, Mother, she wants you to call her. She's very excited, she can't wake Gabriel, and she's afraid."

"Afraid!" Clara stopped because she could hear the rising inflection of her own voice. "What did she say, Tina?" Clara looked around the room, noticed her stole on the bed, and reminded herself that she must not forget it.

"Estela wants you to call her," Tina replied judiciously. Then she added, "Listen, Mother, I think she did not want to frighten me, and you had better call her—"

"OK, don't worry. I'll call her now. Is everything all right with you?"

"With me?" Tina asked. "Sure, why not?"

"All right, dear, won't worry, I'll call Estela now."

She hadn't called Estela in a month, hadn't seen her in six. She put the phone down, reached for the stole, and hugged her shoulders with it. She shivered, and knew she was not cold but fearful. Estela could not wake Gabriel. Alone in that slum apartment in the Bronx, Clara shook herself and dialed the number, surprised that she could remember it. A tiny voice said hello. "Estela, is this you?" Clara asked in Spanish. "Tina called me—"

Like a radio whose volume has suddenly been turned up, the tiny voice became loud. "Clara, Clara, I am all alone!" A sobbing inhalation. "I cannot wake Gabriel! I have rubbed his chest with a hairbrush but he does not wake up—oh, Clara!"

"Estela, listen to me." She paused and heard in her own voice that calm, non-Latin world in which she had lived her adult life. "Estela, have you called a doctor?"

"We have no doctor, my dear. You know how Gabriel was..." Clara noticed the tense, too, and they were both quiet for the quick moment in which they shared the knowledge. "I called the police. I do not know how I remembered those three numbers you see on the telephone booths."

"Listen, Estela, I am taking a taxi immediately—"

"Oh, hurry, my dear—"

"But it may take as much as half an hour to get up to the Bronx. Have you called anyone else?"

"I shall try, I shall try. I have been in the little back bedroom until you called. I do not want to use the phone, for I have only to turn my head and see him sitting in the living room."

"See whom?"

"Gabriel, he was watching television." Her voice had become small again. Then loud: "Why did the children move so far away! I went to bed before he did and he stayed up to watch television and when I woke up, there he was!"

"Estela, I am leaving right now." She head a humming noise on the phone getting louder and louder. "What's that?"

"What?"

"The noise."

"What?" Estela asked again, but Clara recognized the sound of the Bronx elevated subway train and became quiet, as during a visit to Estela and Gabriel, while the rumble and clanging invaded their conversation. And also, as then, their little ground-floor apartment, alarmed and shaken, demanded attention. She saw the small living room filled with cheap versions of French provincial furniture, dominated by a huge television console on which sat painted plaster statuettes of a flamenco dancer and a bullfighter. The double doors next to the TV opened on the front bedroom where, because of lack of space, what was called a bedroom suite seemed stored rather than placed. The living room led to a narrow hall at one end of which stood the shackled door of the apartment—a police lock with its iron bar always in place, and on the edge of the door two locks, each with its chain.

The clatter of the train faded. "Go back to the little bedroom, Estela," Clara said. "I am coming right away." She waited for Estela to hang up first. She heard the click of the phone and thought with terror of Estela running to the back bedroom. It seemed indecent to walk out of this spacious one into a large center hall and stand at the entrance to the long living room and tell them why she must leave immediately. She made her hands into tight fists, as she had done during the last quarrels before her divorce, to control her emotions, to turn them into sane thoughts that can be expressed.

First she had to explain that she had a cousin in the East Bronx. "She is all I have left of my mother's family," she said and saw that her hosts, who were old acquaintances, understood that her cousin Estela was not someone they would have had to dinner. "And I fear that her husband Gabriel is dead," she added. "I must run." She saw them calculate how much help was expected from them and then their relief when Harris said, "I'm coming with you."

She shook her head each time he repeated that, and she explained, "No, I'll manage," but he took her downstairs and left her with the doorman while he went to Broadway and found a taxi. She said no for the last time when he got in it with her. She took his hand by way of thanks and said to the driver, "Southern Boulevard and 170th Street."

The driver moaned, "Oh, lady, I was about to knock off—"

Harris intervened and Clara was again thankful. "I'll make it worth your while—"

"But the Bronx!"

Harris placed a bill in the plastic receptacle where the driver received payment. "I didn't mean that..." the driver said, but the fight had gone out of his voice. "It's dangerous up there this time of night."

"OK, you can put up your off-duty sign when we get off," Harris said. "In fact, if you want, you can ride the arm all the way up there. All right?" His tone and the way he paused for what he expected should be a last agreeable word from the driver would have been impossible for her, and when Harris leaned back after the driver grunted, tears flooded her eyes. Harris put an arm around her and drew her closer, though not intimately, to him, and this seemed to her so much like a moment in a square, romantic movie that she stopped crying.

"I'm OK," she said, but he did not remove his arm. "Do you have a cigarette?" While he took out the cigarettes and she straightened up, the driver asked which route she preferred to the Bronx. "The shortest," she said. "We're trying to beat an ambulance to the place." She turned to Harris. "That's right, an ambulance should be getting there soon—they'll take care of him. There's always a doctor or an intern on them. Why did I have to think the worst just because my cousin found him unconscious? It's my Latin heritage." She shook her head and felt better.

There was room to think of Harris now. "Have you ever been in the Bronx?" she asked.

He nodded.

"I don't mean Riverdale," she said. "I mean *the* Bronx."

"Yes," he said. "Well, not really, just on the expressway, to and from Connecticut."

How to describe it? How to explain about Estela and Gabriel? She remembered—not the fact but the emotion—that she had believed, when she was a girl starting out at school, that it was almost sinful to have a family that spoke Spanish at home. She looked up at Harris as she often had then with teachers and new school friends to see what he made of that. He was waiting, an encouraging smile on his lips, and she felt foolish; she could see he meant only to distract her. She had been right to be attracted to him. He was a nice man.

"They live right in the thickest part of it," she finally said. "Since they married more than 30 years ago. They're more like an aunt and uncle than cousins. Estela is 55 and Gabriel near 60. All these years they have run a little cigar store some two blocks from their apartment, next to the El stairs. Gabriel has been killing himself with that store. Like a peasant on his little plot of land."

"When you say cigar store, do you mean they—"

"Make cigars," she finished for him. "There used to be a lot of stores like that in New York. Besides Estela, Gabriel has a couple of other cigar makers working for him. All old Spaniards like them. I mean, people like them who were born here of Spanish background and who still keep it all in the foreground."

She looked at him and he grinned. She recalled Estela's voice on the phone. What did she mean that she rubbed his chest with a hairbrush? "I'm sorry..." she said. It was their grandmother who suffered from angina and used, when she was short of breath, to brandish the hairbrush while the family gathered around her. "I'm sorry to be dragging you..."

"My great-grandfather was a schoolteacher," Harris said, "my grandfather an insurance salesman, and my father owned a small department store in Alexandria, Ohio. And that makes for a pretty uninteresting background. I'll be happy to meet them."

She nodded, then thought of Gabriel's brother, a cook in a Chelsea restaurant whom she hadn't seen in a few years. "I forgot to ask my cousin if she'd called her brother-in-law," she said. She was now certain Gabriel was dead, and she looked out the taxi window: they were still on the East Side Drive. "Maybe he and his wife are there."

"I didn't mean to sound so jolly and sociological," he said. He picked up her lifeless hand. She nodded; she knew he meant to stop acting like a dinner guest. "Let's not worry until we get there," he said. "OK?"

The taxi, as if on command, swerved off the smooth pavement of the drive onto the broken streets of Harlem. These were new to her; she always took the subway when she went to visit Estela and Gabriel, at Easter or during the summer and always at Christmas. After the El stairs, she stopped at the cigar store to say hello to Gabriel, and he kept her there until they were alone in the store. "Everything all right?" he would ask, meaning, do you need money? And later, at the apartment, Estela would ask the same before Gabriel came home to dinner. "I have my own pennies put away," she would say, as if she'd never said it before. They had helped her generously when she was first establishing herself as a freelance film editor—a profession Estela still called developing pictures—and she could not bring herself to visit them by taxi.

Clara was smiling to herself when she saw that they were only two blocks away. The taxi had stopped in the deserted street for a red light, and she sat forward, frightened as when she first heard Estela on the phone, and tried to peer around the rows of El pillars ahead. Yes, there was a police car double-parked in front of their building and she gripped the handle of the door to be ready to leave as soon as the taxi stopped. "The ground-floor apartment on the right," she said to Harris, and left him to deal with the driver. She ran across the street and said to the policeman standing outside the patrol car, "Have they taken him to the hospital?" and when he did not answer, hurried into the building.

The door to the apartment was open; the lights were on in the hall, the kitchen, and the back bedroom; and all seemed quiet. Clara brought a hand to her heart, remembering this was her own mother's gesture when faced with the unexpected, and stepped inside. A movement made her look into the unlighted living room. A woman with gray hair leaned over Gabriel sitting on the couch directly across from the television set. He was asleep—or unconscious—in his robe and pajamas, his head to one side, one hand clenched on his lap, the other with fingers outspread on the seat of the couch. The woman finished placing a cushion behind his shoulders and then tried to straighten his head.

"Is he better?" Clara asked from the doorway, and the woman turned to her with a start. There were tears on her face and she looked at Clara without moving until she recognized her. "Clara?" she said. Then she slowly shook her head.

"Didn't the ambulance come?" Clara asked.

The woman kept staring at her and Clara realized she was the cigar maker named Lydia who worked for Gabriel. Clara looked at Gabriel again with an effort and this time, more accustomed to the dim light of the room, saw his pallor, a terrible ashen color that she perceived was death. From the back bedroom Estela's voice called, "Who is it? I'm here! Lydia, who is it?" And Clara ran to her. Estela sat in a straight-backed chair wedged between the bed and dresser at the far end of the narrow room. A policeman stood at the foot of the bed.

"Clara!" Estela called. "Would you believe it, the ambulance came and went and they did not take him!"

She looked at the policeman and changed to English. "This is my cousin—please tell her what you said to me."

Clara could not get past the policeman, and she made a gesture to indicate that she wanted to reach Estela. "No, no, speak to him," Estela said. "I am beyond help; I have lived through the worst."

Quietly, respectfully, the policeman turned to Clara. "I've been explaining that the hospital ambulance could not take him because he was already...you know, deceased. If your private doctor comes and signs a death certificate, OK. Otherwise, you will have to wait until the medical examiner comes." He paused and cleared his throat discreetly. "Then you can call the funeral-parlor people. They won't come before."

The policeman looked beyond her and she turned and saw Harris in the doorway. She had forgotten about him.

"There he is, thank God," Estela said.

"No, no," Clara said. "He is a friend who brought me here."

Estela brought her hands together in a supplicating gesture. "Tell him to speak to the policeman," she pleaded. "He is a man."

Clara got past the policeman, and tried to take Estela's hands. "Estela, my dear, what can I do? Tell me."

Estela continued in Spanish. "Tell your friend to speak to the officer. They are men; they will understand each other. And then the ambulance can come and take him away. I cannot stand that he is sitting there without rest."

Clara sat on the bed and put an arm around her, but Estela shook it off. "Do this first," she said. "I do not know how to manage. I had expected that Gabriel would take care of such things—for me."

Clara got up. The police officer was already talking to Harris in the hall, but his back was to the room and she could not hear. When she got to them, she heard him say to Harris, "His private doctor has to have been treating him, you know, during the last 48 hours. You understand?"

"And the medical examiner?" Harris asked.

"My partner already put in a call," the officer said. "But it's Saturday night, you know. They only got one medical examiner in each borough."

Estela called from the bedroom, "The children, Clara, I want you to call the children!" She groaned. "It will take forever." Her voice became small. "They will find their father like that!"

Harris motioned the policeman to the kitchen and Clara returned to Estela. She sat on the bed and noticed that Estela wore a suit and blouse and stockings and shoes.

"Lydia got them for me," Estela explained. "Where is Lydia—oh, there you are."

"Estela, Estela," Lydia said, coming toward her, "you must calm yourself."

"I want to go to the bathroom and I cannot go by there," Estela said, shaking her head to show she wanted no soothing. "No, Lydia, did you look at him like I said? Did it appear to you that one side of his mouth was drawn in? It seemed to me that he pulled it in because he was feeling a terrible pain—like this." She made a grimace. "As if he were wincing. I was asleep. He had been feeling bad all day and he stayed up to watch television because he said he felt better sitting up."

"Do not torture yourself," Lydia said, and with one hand swept tears from her cheeks and then wiped her hand on her dress.

Clara took Estela's hands. "He looks peacefully asleep." Estela's hands did not respond; they were all bones and tendons. "He does."

"You think so?" Estela looked at her dry-eyed and curious, as if she might be inspecting merchandise she was about to buy. "I cannot go in there again. It was different when I was rubbing his chest with the hairbrush but now I cannot, I cannot. And to call the children you have to stand in the hall where the phone is."

Clara said she would call them. "God bless you," Lydia said. "I will get the phone book, because that is something I cannot do. I cannot call those dear children." Clara looked away from the woman to hide her dislike of her forwardness, but Estela did not seem to mind. She said to Lydia, "You know where my little book is, by the phone—bring it to me and I will show Clara."

Lydia left and returned to the doorway immediately. "Your friend wants you," she said to Clara, and she remained in the hallway when Harris, in a low voice, informed Clara that the officer would make no objection if he called a friend who was a doctor to sign the death certificate. "I had to be open with him because by law he has to stay in the apartment until the medical examiner arrives and he would have heard me on the phone," Harris explained.

"What?" Lydia asked, pulling at Clara's dress; her English failed her in moments of excitement. "What doctor?"

Clara put a hand on Harris' arm. "That is very good of you."

"But your cousin," he said. "Ask her if she has any objection."

"Oh, no," Clara said, but she turned back to the bedroom to speak to Estela, Lydia following with the address book. Out of the corner of her eyes Clara saw Gabriel in the living room.

She explained to Estela what Harris meant to do, but it was Lydia who first replied. "Of course, he can," she said. "Isn't that so, Estela? What a fine man. I can see that he knew how to deal with the cop. It must have cost him a few pennies."

Clara shook her head. "It was not like that."

"I must say the ones who come into the store are always looking for a donation," Lydia insisted. "Who can blame them in this neighborhood with all those blacks and Puerto Ricans."

"Tell him that I will be obliged to him, Clara," Estela said, and now she seemed about to cry. "You know what this neighborhood has become—they are out knifing and killing each other all night, and the medical examiner will never get here before the children."

Lydia gave Estela the address book but followed Clara out to the hall. Clara simply nodded to Harris and he picked up the receiver.

Lydia pulled at Clara's dress again. "We cannot leave poor Gabriel like that," she said, and switched to English to speak to the officer who had come to the kitchen door. "It's not good," she said, shaking her head. "Not good like that because his wife wants to go to the bathroom and she will see him." She moved into the living room. "Maybe lying down?"

The officer's voice was firm. "It's not allowed to touch him."

Lydia turned to Clara, her hands clasped before her bosom. "It is asking too much of Estela."

Clara could now look at Gabriel. With Harris on the phone, the horror seemed over. She addressed the policeman. "If we could cover him…"

He nodded. "Oh, that's OK."

"I know where to get a blanket," Lydia said. She walked through the living room to the front bedroom.

Gabriel no longer frightened Clara. She understood why Lydia had wanted to make him comfortable with a cushion. His robe and pajamas were clean and pressed, and she was sure that the bedroom slippers he wore had been polished. Four years ago she and Tina had gone on a Sunday drive and picnic with them and Gabriel's brother and his wife. When they reached the park upstate, there emerged from the trunk of their car a full meal, cold and hot drinks, a grill, charcoal, a tablecloth, and folding chairs. Estela cooked and Gabriel took Tina rowing on the lake. After lunch he had sat under a tree and fallen asleep like this.

Lydia handed her the end of a cotton blanket and together they held it up taut and then allowed it to come down on him gently. His feet were not reached by the blanket, and Lydia leaned down and drew it over them. When she straightened, her eyes were full of tears again. "This is better," she said, "and it is just as well that we did not attempt to move him. Sometimes there is a discharge because all the tension has gone out of the muscles."

Clara checked a movement of distaste. She told herself: That is death and this woman knows how to face it.

"What will happen now?" Lydia said in a voice not meant to carry to the back bedroom, "God only knows. Estela will not be able to keep the store going and that will be the end of my job, three years before social security." She crossed herself and looked at the odd bulk the cotton blanket made on the couch. "If only we could lay him on his side..."

How strange that death should call on one to be practical and efficient. Estela must need her. She turned to the hall and Harris was waiting for her there. He, too, was concerned about practicalities. "I've reached his answering service," he said, "and they promised to have him call here soon."

Lydia was right behind them. "I am going to make coffee," she said. "The officer is sitting there in the kitchen and he will surely want some. What about you and your friend?" Clara nodded. Lydia added in a low voice, "Will your friend drink our coffee? There is no American coffee."

Clara nodded again and noticed that the front door was still open. "Do the police want it open?"

From behind Harris, Lydia signaled her to drop the subject. Puzzled, she went to Estela to get her children's phone numbers. "I heard about the doctor," Estela said, and she managed a little smile, her first; Clara saw that it was one of approval of Harris as a husband. "And listen, Clara, leave the front door open if the policeman does not say anything. It does no harm to keep to the old superstitions."

Clara nodded, but she had never known about that custom. Estela asked her to check that Lydia used the good cups, and she showed her her daughter's phone number in Philadelphia. "You call her first and let her be the one to break the news to her brother in Buffalo," she said. "Men do not take crises well."

"And Gabriel's brother?"

"They went away on vacation, to a farm run by people like us—Spanish," Estela replied. "They will be back tonight, Sunday, so they will learn in plenty of time. I don't want to have their last morning ruined and then have to drive into the city nervous."

Clara sat with the address book in her hand and looked at Estela with love and worry. Estela said, "Go and make the call. Try not to frighten her, for you will be waking her. Poor girl… But it has to be."

Clara made the phone call under the worst circumstances. First, she had to wait, once she reached Estela's daughter, for the noise of an El train to stop. Then a woman whom she recognized as the second cigar maker in Gabriel's store appeared with her husband at the front end of the hall and began to scream as she rushed with arms outstretched toward her. She stopped when she saw it was not Estela at the phone, and instead embraced Lydia as she came out of the kitchen. The husband held his hat in his hand and looked at the bulk on the living room couch. He said to Harris in Spanish, "I knew it would be like this—my wife's nerves are very delicate and Estela and Gabriel are like brother and sister to her, sister and brother."

"I am here! I am here!" Estela called from the bedroom and the new arrival rushed there, her voice rising as she passed Clara and reaching a near scream in the bedroom. It was suddenly muffled. Clara heard her sobbing, and was irritated that she was so much noisier and demonstrative than Estela or her daughter who had gasped, become quiet, and then businesslike. Clara hurried the call and went into the bedroom to protect Estela from the woman. She found them in each other's arms and Estela crying with the kind of release that she knew from her Spanish childhood in Chelsea was supposed to be good for you.

"He was so good to us, Estela," the woman said. "There was no one who did not know his goodness."

"Yes, yes," Estela replied, "Yes, yes."

It seemed to Clara that Estela had lost her poise and good sense.

"Here is your young cousin," the woman continued. "She knows how good Gabriel was. Am I lying? Was he not a good, good man?"

"Yes," Clara said, but her voice was as strangled as her feelings and she backed out of the room. She studied Harris in the doorway of the kitchen. The woman's husband talked to him now in English. The man had found a bottle of Spanish cognac and he held it up, urging Harris to lace his demitasse with it. Lydia stuck her head out into the hall and beckoned Clara into the kitchen.

"Do you want coffee or tea?" she asked. "Each has its uses. I am so glad that Marta has come." Clara gathered that was the woman's name. "She has a good effect on Estela—it was not good for her to hold it all in. This is much better—let her cry."

The policeman sat at the kitchen table and looked worried about the demitasse of coffee Lydia had served him. Clara sat across from him and they nodded at one another. She stole a glance at Harris and it seemed to her that he was enjoying himself, nodding and nodding at Marta's husband as he sipped his coffee. Clara minded but did not know why. He saw her looking his way and his face became serious and questioning, offering his help. She tried to appear grateful and to shake her head at the same time. He came over, leaned a hand on the table, and lowered his head to hers. "Is there anything you want done?" he asked. "Please tell me." Lydia, the policeman, and Marta's husband all watched with approval, as if they were privileged to be with superior beings.

Harris must know that his actions made it appear to Spaniards that he was committed to her in the traditionally affianced way. Or, if they thought ill of her, that she was his mistress. She covered her face with one hand. She did not want to laugh. The phone rang and like the others she watched Harris go to the hall to answer it. It was all going to be over now.

“Lydia said, “God provides, God provides,” then added, “I found a chicken in the refrigerator and I am going to make soup. There is nothing so fortifying.”

Clara could not make out what Harris was saying on the phone and got up to be with him when he finished. He appeared in the door of the kitchen with a look of consternation and shame. “He won't come—the son of a bitch!”

Clara groaned involuntarily and then touched his arm to reassure him. Estela called from the bedroom and she went to her.

“Is the doctor coming?” Estela asked.

Clara shook her head. Harris called from behind her, “I am sorry; he is no friend after all.”

Estela and Marta looked blank. Then Estela began to moan, “Aiee, aiee, aiee, I can wait no longer. I cannot, I cannot.” Marta got up and motioned to Clara to go out to the hall. “I shall cover you,” she said to Estela, and put her arms around her. “You will not have to see anything.”

In the hall Clara pulled Harris to her and together they blocked the door of the living room. The others stood in the door of the kitchen, turning the hall into a closed tunnel from the bedroom to the bathroom. Estela came out of her room with her head down and her shoulders hunched. “Aiee, aiee, aiee,” she moaned as she went by. No one spoke. When the bathroom door closed, Lydia said, “Poor girl,” but no one replied and they all remained at their posts. In a moment the door opened and Estela called, “Marta, Marta, walk ahead of me, for the love of God!” She paused before the door of the living room and breathed so loud that it seemed to Clara that she was talking in this strange way to Gabriel. Marta pulled at her hands and she began to squeal, "Aiee, aiee," and shuffle to the bedroom.

"I'm sorry," Harris said to Clara when they were alone. "I acted like such a big deal, they must be disappointed in me."

She shook her head. "No, they always expect the worst." In a second she added, "Me, too." Then she smiled. "Look, you've been very kind but you don't have to stay any longer. They have many friends and they'll be coming from all over the city..."

"I'll take you home when you're ready."

"Me?" Then she saw the man in the baggy suit standing in the doorway of the apartment. He looked like a character in a 1930s' movie and she knew he was the medical examiner.

"Where's the deceased?" the man asked, rolling his cigar butt from one corner of his mouth to the other. He looked into the kitchen, saw the policeman, and exclaimed, "Hey, Larry, what's the story!"

"In here," Harris said, and motioned him to the living room. The examiner looked at him with curiosity. Harris added, "Heart attack."

"You a doctor?" the examiner asked, and did not wait for an answer. The officer followed him. "You can thank your lucky stars you pulled this one—you should of seen the last one. What a night!"

Clara moved away when they tugged at the cotton blanket. She went to Estela and told her the medical examiner had arrived.

Estela took her hands to hold her there. "Make sure, Clara, that you get Cooke's. I don't want the Puerto Rican funeral parlor. Call Cooke's now and before that man leaves let him talk to them on the phone so they will come right away." She paused. "The children should be here in two hours at most." She reached up and for the first time hugged Clara. "Clara, Clara, oh, my dear, you are like my own child."

When Estela let go of her, Clara was blind with tears. She bumped into Harris in the doorway. "I'll take care of this," he said, and went to the phone. "I know what she wants. Go back to her."

She went back inside and sat on the bed. With Marta and Estela she listened to Harris talking to Cooke's and waited for the examiner. She got up to give the address to Harris, and the examiner came into the hall at the same time.

"Where's the wife?" he said. "No foul play here."

"No foul play!" she exclaimed. "What do you mean! Is that why we have been put through this—so you can decide there's been no foul play!"

"Aw, come on, lady!" the policeman said. "*You* ought to understand."

"I don't understand," Clara said. "I'm no different than anyone here."

She saw Harris hold up the phone and touch the medical examiner's arm. She turned and went to Estela. She heard Harris saying, "I would be very obliged to you, very obliged, if you would speak to Cooke's right now..." Something in his voice irked her. He took sides with the medical examiner and the policeman, and she knew he would get his way. When the examiner came into the bedroom, he winked at her, as if congratulating her about Harris, and he said, "Everything's on track. It's just routine."

"OK," he continued, after he too sat on the bed and took out a pen and some forms. "Who is going to interpret? I've got to get a few facts from the lady here."

Estela straightened. "Ask me and I'll tell you," she said in English.

They were not through with the forms when Clara saw Harris beckoning. There were two men with a stretcher in the living room. Harris whispered, "They're ready to take him as soon as the examiner gives them the paper. Do you think we should tell your cousin?"

Lydia decided for them. She squeezed past them, calling Estela as she went, but Estela would not come out. First out of the back bedroom came the medical examiner, then Lydia and Marta. Harris and she had to make way. Harris went into the living room and Clara stood in the door of the kitchen. Marta's husband leaned toward her and she could smell the liquor on his breath. "Your friend gave them all money; that is why it is being done so quickly." She followed his gaze and saw the stretcher emerging from the living room. Gabriel was covered with a sheet but it could not hide that his body was locked in a sitting position, as awkward as a show-window dummy. To maneuver the hall the two men tilted the stretcher and she first noticed the straps holding him down. Gabriel was not insubstantial and the men were panting as they went by her.

The others followed the stretcher to the street, and Harris stopped by her as he, too, went out. "Just a couple of words with them," he said, "and I'll be back for you."

She looked puzzled and he realized his mistake. "I thought you might want to leave now," he explained, "and come back later."

She shook her head. "You've been very kind," she began, and suddenly decided to act herself. She kissed and hugged him quickly. "Go now, you've done enough." She saw the happiness in his eyes and also saw him think that she was a Latin after all and this pleased her.

In the bedroom, Estela was hunched. She covered her face with both hands. When Clara sat on the bed, she brought them down. "I cannot go in there yet," she said, and reached out to squeeze Clara's arm. "But I can tell you where the clothes are that I want you to send to Cooke's for him to wear. I do not want the children to have to think about that. I thank God you are here. There will be a lot of people and a lot of work to do."

The American Sickness

The flight to Montevideo that Ellie's mother was taking left from Kennedy Airport, and the drive down from Adams College in Massachusetts provided the two of them with the opportunity of passing on final instructions to one another. It was also one of the two, sure, annual occasions—coming from and going to Montevideo—when her mother felt the inclination to chat to no purpose. She had been flying up every spring and staying until school opened in the fall before returning to her older daughter in Uruguay. She had been doing this for five years, since Ellie and her husband separated, but it was such a minor complication in her life that Mercedes (Ellie had been taught to call her mother by her first name during the Nazi occupation of France) was surprised when Ellie said in Spanish, "You must wish sometimes that life were simpler."

"My life or your life?" Mercedes said. "Or your son's?"

Ellie always listened to Mercedes from the stance of a detached, friendly observer, and Mercedes' response made her laugh. "Let's not talk about *my* life," she said. "And your grandson is a regular American boy."

"Well, my life could not be simpler," Mercedes said, and reached forward and pushed the ashtray on the dashboard closed. "I married one man and stayed with him."

Ellie laughed louder. “What a bitch you are!”

“This country has ruined your manners,” Mercedes replied, “Profanity is for men.”

“You’ve never left Saragossa,” Ellie said, “and yet we have changed countries more often than our shoes.”

“You exaggerate, as usual,” Mercedes said. “It was two or three countries and no more.”

Ellie said, “A German poet said that.”

“German!” Mercedes said, and smiled the austere smile that Ellie called her Castilian, aristocratic smile. “They traveled because they wanted to.”

“A good German, Mercedes,” Ellie said, and Mercedes sighed as if calling on some absent authority to confirm that her doubts about Germans were not unreasonable. “And it *was* four countries,” Ellie insisted, “Spain, France, Uruguay, the United States.”

“Speak for yourself,” Mercedes said, and looked quickly at, and then away from, Hartford, which Ellie herself admitted was ridiculous. “I am only visiting this country.”

“Mercedes!” Ellie exclaimed. “It is your grandchild’s fatherland!”

“Ah, yes,” Mercedes said, and stroked her patent leather pocketbook as if she had won the argument.

Well, for me it’s four countries, Ellie thought; and last year in Brazil, that’s five.

“You cannot remember Spain,” Mercedes said, pursuing her own argument. “You were two in 1937 when we crossed the International Bridge at Hendaye.”

“How many times do I have to tell you, Mercedes, that I do remember!” Ellie said. “Irun was on fire.”

"You remember your father's stories."

Ellie said, "May he rest in peace."

Mercedes hugged her before going on the plane and got to the point Ellie had hoped to head off. "What do I tell them when I get there? Will you take the post at the university?"

"If I went back," Ellie said, "I'd join the Eupamaros."

"Elvira, God forbid!" Mercedes exclaimed, using Ellie's Spanish name. "You know they are holding the position open for you. I shall tell them you accept and will come in June, and the devil with these yearly trips of mine."

"No, no," Ellie said hurriedly. "Tell Don Diego that I shall write and give him my decision."

"It is an American sickness, this not making up one's mind," Mercedes said. "Don't kiss me if you do not mean to come."

"Mercedes, I shall kiss you no matter what." Once on each cheek, while Mercedes closed her eyes enduring her. "Give my sister my love."

Mercedes lifted her eyebrows to indicate she was exasperated.

Ellie said, "Maybe I shall come."

"You are still my same little chicken—with its head cut off," her mother replied, and turned quickly to the man waiting to check her ticket.

Going back, Ellie did not drive into New York City. Too tempting, and stopping at the lawyer's for the final papers might make her feel bad. She was half committed to a party at the Dawsons' that night, and there was Jason—he was still only ten-years old and he shouldn't be left to eat alone the very day his grandmother left. She drove over the Triborough Bridge without any trouble—it was two in the afternoon and traffic was manageable—but she had to slow down often and stop altogether a couple of times in the Bronx where, it seemed to her, the unfinished approach to the Connecticut Turnpike had been in a state of repair and indecision for years. "They don't know what they're doing," she said aloud. "Like me."

And she pondered again, now that Mercedes was out of the way, whether she should devote the school year to finishing her history of Brazil or to completing the translation of Clarin's *La Regenta*. Both projects were financed by grants—one from the Ford Foundation, the other from the National Translation Center—and she assuaged her guilt at accepting them simultaneously by recalling her Brazilian friends' encouragement last summer: "Take all you can get out of those Yankees—it will never be more than a tiny bit of what they have stolen from us."

"But I shall have to decide one of these days whether I am a literary historian or a political historian," she said brightly as she approached the first toll, where the man in the booth seeing her lips move asked, "What?"

"Lovely day," she said.

"Yeah?"

"Yes!" she insisted, and drove off laughing. They refuse to play their part, she thought; they do not have the Latins' sense that we must keep one another's spirits up. Such an insistently unhappy people. It was then she remembered the visiting lecturer two years ago who had told her she was like a Viennese torte.

"A Viennese torte!" she had said, delighted. "What kind—with fruit and nuts?"

"Oh, I guess I mean what we call a seven-layer cake here," he said. She nodded and he took heart to continue. "There's so much to one that you can lift a part of the cake from the rest and each section is a cake in itself."

The face of the lecturer blurred in her memory with those of men and women at cocktail parties looking puzzled when she was introduced as Ellie Smith. The faces cleared when she explained that until she married her name was Elvira Zaitegui. The puzzlement began again when they realized her accent was French. At that point she recited her resume; it put them at ease and gave her something to talk about.

"The Zaitegui is Spanish Basque," she would begin. "At the age of two, when Franco took the north of Spain, I crossed over into France in my mother's arms. We lived there for nine years and then we went to Uruguay because Spain was out of the question. I went to school and college in Montevideo; married an American—therefore, Smith; and came to New York where I worked at my master's and also my doctorate at Columbia." She'd pause as if for questions, then add, "All very ordinary," and laugh with more pleasure than any Professor Smith would have.

Sometimes she was obliged to tell more. There was always more, for only fools thought her experience was ordinary—indeed, their response to her statement was a useful test—but she could never tell all. There were bits and pieces of her life that she forgot for months at a time or that friends didn't learn until long after they had become intimate. It was only after she divorced her husband that it occurred to her that he did not know why she called her mother Mercedes. Had she withheld it because of what it told about her? During the Nazi occupation, her father had been hid in a warehouse in Bordeauz, and she was taught to say Mercedes because the French family who had taken them in hoped that if her mother was sent away to a camp they could save Ellie by claiming her as their own. That was how Madame Paillard became—suddenly, as everything in her life—Maman. Yes, to have told her husband might have made her seem emotionally dependent, which she feared she was, and she had wanted to be helpful, no burden to him: therefore, the degrees and the teaching she undertook, which he considered competitive. Ay, ay, Americans, she thought, what are their hidden experiences?

There was only one experience she purposely kept to herself. The young graduate student in Brazil who stayed in her apartment for two weeks. One member of the five-man underground cell to which he belonged had been picked up by the police, and that meant that the other four had to disperse and stay under cover until they learned whether the one who was caught had talked. They usually talked. Pedro expected that his comrade would. He expected, too, that when it came time to leave her apartment he would have to lead a totally clandestine life in some other city, and he began to prepare for it by growing a mustache, reshaping his eyebrows, and shaving the hairline of his forehead to give himself a wide brow. "Goodbye to the College of Engineering," he said to her when the transformation was done. "Look at me, wouldn't you say I belong in Arts and Letters?"

She slept with him the day that she came home at midday from the National Archives, where she spent most days doing research, to give him the message, delivered to her there, that at seven that evening a car would be waiting for him on Copacabana. He was alone in the apartment when she told him. Mercedes had taken Jason to friends in Leblon to play on the beach and Ellie was to meet them for dinner there. "You thrive on all those old documents," her hostess announced when Ellie finally arrived that evening at Leblon, looking happy. "My, you're radiant!" And Ellie quickly greeted the others there.

"No, no," interrupted a young journalist with whom her friend had taken to pairing her. "It is Rio that does it—being away from that terrible country up north!"

Ellie's friend shook her head. "You are wrong—she is a Yankee and likes to work."

"I am three-quarters of an hour late," Ellie said. "How can you say I am a Yankee?"

Pedro had been simply and direct. Sleeping with him was akin to the care that Mercedes had taken of him for two weeks: his laundry was done at home, separately, to avoid suspicion; there was coffee on the stove for him at all hours. He hugged Ellie in excitement when she gave him the message, and then he asked her. Later, walking past the two doormen on duty in the lobby, she enjoyed the irony that only this once were they right about the divorced woman who went out alone so often. "When they see a woman and a man together," she said to Pedro in the car, "politics is the last thing on their minds. Like all you Brazilians. So be sure to kiss me goodbye when I drop you off."

But she kept her eyes on the rearview mirror as he leaned toward her and kissed her, and she noticed that the man in the car to which Pedro was transferring studied the sidewalk and the shop entrances. She waited until they drove away. Nothing happened that was not planned, and she arrived at her friends' in Leblon feeling so good because she felt supremely useful. Still, Pedro, who was twelve years younger than she, had his effect: the journalist, the naval officer, the librarian in the days that followed almost persuaded her in their different ways. It was her last month in Rio, but she held out: no, no, no, she had picked up the notion on the other side of Hendaye, an old Spanish prejudice nursed by Mercedes, that a divorced woman was a bad woman, and she was not going to live up to the part.

Behind the wheel now, she shook her head at her summer's recollection and saw in the disappointed face of the girl in dungarees, who stood by the last New Haven exit on the turnpike holding a placard that said ADAMS, that she had turned down a hiker. A girl, too. She braked, moved onto the graveled edge of the road and started to back up. In the rearview mirror she saw the dungareed figure sprint toward her car: it was a boy. She was tempted to take off again but remembered he was an Adams' student. She'd be safe and, anyway, she needed a companion to keep her from reminiscing.

The boy looked in the window first, shook the long hair off his brows, and said, "Hi, Mrs. S.!"

"You!" she exclaimed, and quickly remembered his name. "Sandy Lands."

He settled into the seat next to hers, looked at her with a fair face that radiated wonder, and said, as she took off, "Wow, doesn't it blow your mind!"

"Gibberish," she replied. "Don't talk gibberish to me. If you mean that this is an extraordinary coincidence—"

"What else?"

"Then you shouldn't be so happy about it. I'm the last person you want to run into."

"Never, Mrs. S." He looked serene. "You're not one of the deadies," he explained, and maneuvered two fingers into the pocket of his dungarees to extract a cigarette.

"You didn't register this fall, you didn't take my finals last spring—"

"I'm down on myself about that," he said, but didn't look unhappy. "I was going straight to your house to rap—to discuss it with you. You know, get the lay of the land."

"Oh, you want to be taken back?" she said, saw him begin the same search in his pockets for matches, and pointed to the lighter on the dashboard and pushed it in for him. "If that's a joint, I'm driving you straight to a police station."

"Ho, ho, I remember when you called them pigs," he said. "It's great to run into you like this. I was afraid you didn't come back from Brazil." He leaned back, relaxed, as if all his problems were solved. He held up the cigarette. "It's only a squashed Camel."

"I don't know why I did," she said without thinking.

"Yeah," he said, and she knew that he must be looking at her with great seriousness. She glanced at him, to check. Third World, his innocent eyes said. "It's real down there," he said.

"Romantic nonsense," she replied. "You know I am a bourgeois liberal."

"God, Mrs. S., I apologized about that." His voice was small and aggrieved. "I was stoned that night; I never told you."

"Sandy!"

The snow had melted the day spring officially began when the students, Sandy prominently among them, occupied the administration building and the student center. Their first act was to paint "Ho lives" on the token piece of marble above the wide glass doors of the center, a modern building; they couldn't bring themselves to deface the fake Gothic of the administration building, and there were many discussions later about that. Their second act was to issue, on the best paper in the president's office, their list of demands, all copied from Berkeley and Columbia. Gayle Dawson, Ellie's department head, a man who had been expelled from the Communist Party in 1932 as a Trotskyist, was the first to show the mimeographed statement to her. "Workers and peasants of the Bronx, unite," he said.

She had to laugh but she didn't want to. She feared politics; it brought civil war, torture, exile; it was the cause of her father's unhappy life. The last ten years he taught in a Catholic girls' school in Montevideo, and when he died, an exile Republican newspaper carried an article about him. He died on a Wednesday, was buried on Friday, was lauded in the weekly paper on Saturday, and on Sunday afternoon the Jesuit head of the school came to visit them. Was it true, he asked, that Sr. Zaitegui had been an atheist and a Red? She was the youngest in the room and the question was not directed to her. "He swallowed his pride to work for you," she had volunteered, taking her stand on politics. "To free us he was willing to forget about politics, which you people are not generous enough to do." In her mind she classed the Jesuit priest with Gayle Dawson, and her father with the students. She felt rather than perceived the connection, and all she could say to Dawson when he showed her the demands of the strikers was, "I'm worried about my students."

The students stayed in the buildings not quite forty-eight hours. On the second evening came the bust. When news of it reached her, she was meeting with some of the younger faculty members who hoped to mediate between the students and the administration. They all rushed to the campus. Ellie sobbed when she saw Sandy being dragged into a police van. This is madness, she thought, I didn't feel this bad when my marriage broke up.

She brought herself under control and tried to think of a way to be useful. She must get to the police station and see that they were not mistreated. The police chief was her next-door neighbor, and with mixed deference, fatherliness and self-importance, he escorted her and a young Sinologist into the small town jail. The cells were jammed and the noise let up enough when they walked in for Ellie to hear Sandy clearly: "Here come the bourgeois liberals expiating their guilt!" followed by the chanting, deafening in that confined corridor, "Pigs, pigs, pigs!"

"Everybody apologized to you, Mrs. S.," Sandy said. "Like we didn't know then you don't go into action stoned."

"So what do you know now?" Ellie said.

"Hey, you're tough," he replied. "But I knew that."

She looked at him out of the corner of an eye, and he caught her at it. They broke into laughter together.

"What if I told you I know how to put together a time bomb?" he said.

"I'd say you were crazy," she answered, and involuntarily accelerated the car. "But first of all, you wouldn't tell me, right?"

"No," he said, but he didn't sound convincing. She looked at him again, and again they laughed. "Why are you coming back to Adams?" she asked. "I thought all the activists were leaving the campuses."

"I want to become a doctor," he said. "I was up at a commune in Vermont all summer. What the Movement needs is doctors, lawyers, technicians."

"What?"

"Service skills," he explained.

"Technicians..." she began.

Sandy interrupted, "Electrical engineers who—"

"Don't tell me!" She took a hand off the wheel and waved it at him. "I don't want to know." They were approaching Hartford, and she kept up her warning hand. "Don't talk to me now anyway or I'll get into the wrong lane."

When she was on 91, she asked, “Did you see the Mark Twain house?”

He looked blank.

“Remember in your liberal arts days—I told you about it. Harriet Beecher Stowe lived in Hartford. A center of radical abolitionists and feminists, then of the gilded-age nouveau riches,” she explained, and suppressed a smile because she sounded like the notes she kept on file cards.

“Oh, yeah, yeah,” he said.

“So?”

“I figured it was no log cabin.”

“All right, half an hour and we'll be home,” she said in her classroom voice. “Are you willing to make some apologies?”

“I'll do my best with the registrar and department heads,” she explained, “but once I've felt them out, you're going to have to come along with me and convince them you're serious. Dawson is on the disciplinary committee—”

“Oh, God,” he said.

“Sandy—”

“No, no, I'll say anything you want. I'll look as straight as the dean; I've got other duds up there…”

“You've got a place for tonight then?”

“Oh, I can crash a lot of pads,” he replied.

“Good, I'll talk to Dawson tonight—” she chuckled to think this was what convinced her to go to the party—“and you see me in my office tomorrow morning.”

“When?” he asked.

"You just camp there early and wait—in fear and trembling."

"You Spaniards are really groovy," he said. His way of thanking her.

"Romantic nonsense," she replied.

◇

The light was on in the foyer when Ellie picked up the mail at the table by the door. "Jason! Jason!" she called.

His voice, ostentatiously well-modulated, answered from the living room, just a few steps away. "I'm here," he said. He was lying on his back on the floor, his legs up on the coffee table. The TV was on but the sound was not. "Waiting for the five o'clock news, Ellie," he added, letting her see the remote control in his hand.

"It's hardly sunset and you've got the lights on," she said. "All over the house, too, I bet."

"I know what you're thinking," he said. "But I'm not scared. It's just a reflex—I turn them on automatically when I go into a room, honest."

"Don't you want to know about Mercedes?" she said, shuffling the letters she had gathered and noticing there was one for her mother from her sister in Montevideo.

"What about Mercedes?" he asked. "There's a swell offer from Time magazine—nine cents an issue."

"She's your grandmother," Ellie replied. "Don't you want to know if she got off all right?"

"Well, obviously, for Christ's sakes," he said, and threw out his free hand and let it fall on the floor above his head.

Ellie perched on the arm of a chair and stopped looking through the letters. "Now, listen, I want you, now that Mercedes isn't here to do it, to call me Elvira," she said. "Otherwise, I'll forget who I am."

"Okay, but none of that Javier stuff for me—you call me Jason," he replied. "I tell you what, you and I can switch to Spanish now and give the French a rest."

She didn't answer, instead cocked an ear towards the foyer and stairs. "Jason, I hear the radio in your room going."

Jason swung a leg off the coffee table and turned on the sound of the TV with the remote-control gadget.

"Jason!" Ellie called.

"What! What!" he replied, louder than she.

"Go upstairs and turn it off."

"Why?"

"Because I'm going upstairs to lie down a moment before I prepare dinner and I don't want to have the radio blaring—"

Jason covered his eyes with one hand, in exasperation. "You're going upstairs—what's to prevent you from turning it off?"

"Because I'm not going into your filthy room!" She got up, the mail in one hand, her pocketbook in other. "Besides, it's a punishment. You go up and turn it off now before the five o'clock news—"

He dashed ahead of her and she met him again on the stairs coming down. "Stay out of my room," he said.

"A pleasure," she said.

She threw off her shoes without bending to ease them off, and then crossed to her bed. She placed the mail on the night table and reminded herself that she should, as soon as she changed, take the mail to her study across the landing. Everything in its place. She pulled off her dress and lay in bed in her half-slip; she threw her arms out limply to relax. Now that Mercedes was gone, she must make sure to be neat—hang the clothes when she got up from this rest, find her shoes, straighten the bed—and not continue as the sloppy adolescent girl that she became when Mercedes visited. Her dependency. She smiled and pushed away the thought. "I'm not turning into an American," she said to the stain on the ceiling. "No worrier, she." She then repeated this in French, Spanish, Italian, Portuguese, enjoying the effort it took her with each to find the equivalent for the American construction of no-worrier-she.

She thought of Mercedes' parting words and rolled her head on the pillow from side to side: she did not want to think about leaving this country. No. New-term jitters, that's what her complaining had been. The letter from her sister Clara. She reached for it, opened it (messily, she chided herself) and learned without warning that Pedro was dead. Tortured to death by the secret police.

"Mom, Mom!" Jason called up the stairwell. "What do you want?"

She was sitting at the edge of the bed. She must have screamed. Her throat hurt and she heard the sound she'd made reverberating in her head now, like an echo. She tried to swallow, in order to answer Jason, and instead began to sob.

"Listen, Mom," Jason continued, "I'll clean it up later. Okay?"

"Okay," she called and crooked her arm over her face to stop the howl that threatened to follow. She remained on the edge of the bed hunched over, trying to remember Pedro's face, and watched her tears fall on her knees. The sound of the television reached her. She was used to watching the afternoon news with Jason and she straightened as reflex. "He's not news," she said to herself to explain why she didn't get up, and the thought helped her. She wiped her face with one hand and with the other took up her sister's letter again. "When I see you I'll tell you how we got the news from Brazil, but meanwhile I thought Elvira would want to know," her sister ended. Along the margin she added, "His body has not been returned."

After a while she walked across the landing to the bathroom. She must think about dinner. As she walked into the bathroom she said, "And what am I doing in this miserable country?"

The only boy with short hair in her freshman class had said yesterday, "It seems to me, Mrs. Smith, that you always imply that we're responsible for every unfortunate thing that happens in Latin America."

"Miserable country," she repeated, and bent over the washbasin and threw water on her face to keep from crying again. There was no one she could talk to about Pedro. She would not go to the Dawsons' party. She would heat the chickpea pottage her mother had cooked and make pepper steak with the leftover roast beef. If she went to the party, she might talk about Pedro and she knew that later she would be sorry. What did they know about young men like him? She thought: he would not talk and that's why they tortured him to death. She sat on the edge of the bathtub while she absorbed that thought.

On the way to the kitchen, she passed the foyer and Jason said, "Okay if I have my dinner here?" She did not answer and he took it as a good sign. During a commercial he ran into the kitchen and told her there had been a call from Mrs. Dawson in the afternoon. "They've got a party at their house or something."

"I hope you weren't definite," Ellie said. "I don't know if I can go."

"Well, I told her it wouldn't be because of me," he replied. "I mean, you can't use that excuse anymore, Mom." He noticed the bottle of soy sauce on the stove, and added, "Wow, pepper steak!"

His exclamation reminded her of Sandy. If she didn't go the party and talk to Dawson about him, she would not have much advice for Sandy when he came by the office in the morning. What had she planned to say to Dawson? How to convince him of Sandy's seriousness now? Tell him that Sandy meant to work hard because the Movement needed doctors and lawyers and electrical engineers who could put together a bomb? She chuckled as she stirred the pottage—this might be just the thing to tickle Dawson into helping Sandy. Then she thought of Pedro and was ashamed that she could so soon be distracted from mourning him. She lay down the spoon, checked that Jason had left the kitchen, and quickly crossed herself, completing the gesture by bringing her closed hand to mouth and kissing the thumbnail.

Ordinary Things

"Ordinary things," Melinda said. "They're really important."

She stopped and waited and, as usual, would not start up again unless she had your complete agreement.

I didn't much care, but I nodded. Enough to convince her she had my undivided attention. What did I have to lose?

Melinda and I had grown up this way, she talking, me listening, since we first met in seventh grade in George Washington Junior High School. George Washington has been closed and boarded up and derelict for at least twenty years. Ten years before that, a good ten years, it was used as a warehouse for the public school system. This should give you an idea of how old Melinda and I are, and the state we are in.

Melinda did not get to finish her thought right away, for once, the way she always does with me. A car new to our block parked behind me at the curb, and I wished we could shift our attention to it. I did not know its driver was one of Melinda's grandsons—one of the bunch that is half cracker—but she did, and still she wanted to finish her thought. It was making me nervous. A strange car on the block. That is what Tampa has become: you cannot turn your back on anyone you do not personally know.

"Hey," the fellow called.

It gave me a chance to take a good look. He was a youngster. Probably not yet twenty, but you cannot tell about American boys like that. They are skinny and smooth-skinned, and even when everything about them, wet hair and all, tells you they have just taken a shower they do not look clean. Not really clean the way we Latins do. They are going to look that way at sixty, stringy, with a skimpy potbelly, all slicked down with spit not soap and hot water. It was really his voice that told me he was a teen-ager. There was something innocent about it.

"Are you Mrs. Lopez?" he said.

Should I just tell him I was not and see what he had to say?

Melinda snapped her fingers in frustration at not being able to finish her thought.

"What makes you think Mrs. Lopez wants to talk to you?" she said. "You had ten years you could've come by and said, hello, Grandma, how are."

"I'll be darned," he said, and I could hear that he had censored his speech for our sakes. A good sign. "You're Grandma," he said, "and you knew me?"

"I saw your mother looking at me at the Public Market last week," Melinda said. "I figured one of you would be showing up any day now."

He got out of the car. He was much taller standing. "Hey," he said again. "Was I there?"

"I saw she was on food stamps," Melinda said. "What does she want?"

"I didn't see you," he said, and stopped at the cement on the sidewalk, confused. "I don't know what she wants," he said. He waited, but there was something in his stance that said I'm not waiting long, I won't stay if I am not welcome.

"I suppose you want a big greeting," Melinda said. "Like you were in Viet Nam." It was now she who waited.

He looked down. She was not what he expected. He was tall but he was feeling small.

"Go hug her," I said.

He looked at her to see what she thought of that.

"Come on," Melinda said. "I want a kiss, too."

She opened her arms and I could have died with delight. They hugged and hugged right there on the grass. Melinda talks and talks, but it's me that knows what she wants.

"Here," she said to me. "You hug him a while now—I'm gonna make him some iced tea."

He went right for me as if this was what he had expected when he looked up his Latin grandmother in Ybor City. Kindly old ladies and lots of hugging. I liked doing it; he smelled good. Maybe he didn't use soap and water; maybe he came by his perfume naturally. Like my husband had.

"Or do you want a Coke?" she said.

"I'll take the iced tea," he said.

We heard the screen door across the street slam closed and we both turned to look. It was Herminia, of course.

"Wouldn't you know," Melinda called. "You got the best nose for gossip in all Ybor City."

Herminia spoke up in her sweet voice. "Don't you believe her, young man, I'm not like that."

"He's not a young man, he's my grandson," Melinda said, then tried another joke: "His name is Sean, I think. Ha-ha! I'm the old lady who lived in a shoe. Who can keep track? These crackers have whole litters at a time. Sean, right? Speak up."

Herminia doubled up on her porch.

"You wanna make something of it?" he said, catching on himself. "Juan, right?"

We laughed; he had such a cracker accent.

"You want a sandwich?" Melinda said. "I got all kinds of cold cuts. Cold pork, too. You know about cold pork, Cuban style?"

Herminia spoke up for him as if he needed a reference. "He knows Sean is Juan in Spanish," she said.

I felt like getting in there myself and saying I knew, too, but I don't believe in competing.

Herminia started down her steps.

"You stay there, Herminia," Melinda said. "I haven't talked to him in a decade—a decade, isn't that something? You talk to him another day. Or ten years from now if me and him have a fight. Are we gonna have a fight?"

The boy kept turning from one of us to the other but mostly stared at Melinda. He was not swatting us off, but he was acting as if he had walked into a beehive.

"What do you want?" Melinda said to him. "Huh?"

Herminia went back to her porch, disappointed, but I followed Melinda and Sean inside. I did not even think about it. I mean, since our husbands died, Melinda and I were closer than when we were teen-agers, and that's close.

On the way to the kitchen, Sean looked around. "You live here by yourself, Grandma?"

"Yes, and that's the way I like it," she said. She gestured in my direction. "Sylvia here lives next door. She's got the whole house to herself, too."

He looked at me, and I nodded.

"How do you like that name, Sylvia?" she asked him. "Used to be a pretty common name; now it sounds fancy."

For once I objected. "What about Melinda?" I said.

"I like your name, ma'am," he said to me. To Melinda: "I like it. You were gonna have iced tea yourself?"

"What makes you think that?" Melinda asked.

We were all three standing in the doorway of the kitchen, and she asked the question as if it were an important matter that had to be decided. "Did I say I want iced tea?"

He shrugged. "I don't know, didn't you?"

"You don't want it?" Melinda said.

"Not if you don't want it, Grandma," he said.

I knew how he was feeling: confused. Melinda does that to you. I made faces to let him know he should pay no mind, but he did not see me. It made me feel a little foolish, but not too much so.

"I thought you might like iced tea to help you get that sandwich down, honey," she said. "I can take it or leave it."

"Why'm I having the sandwich?" he said.

"He's your grandson, Melinda, I can see that," I said. "He can ask more questions than you."

"You got my number," he said to me.

Melinda raised her voice to drown us out. "Cause boys are supposed to eat, that's why," she said. "What else you gonna do here?"

He looked at her and cocked his head and looked at her some more and then at me. He winked at me as if we had an understanding about Melinda. We did: she's a character.

He took the two or three steps into the kitchen to get to the table and looked back at her for permission.

"Go ahead, sit down," she said. "So your mother didn't send you?"

He shook his head. "Did my father speak Spanish all the time?" he said.

"That is a very strange thing to say," I said.

"Well, he could have," Melinda said. "If he wanted, he could have. I can speak Spanish all the time."

"And say everything you want to say?" he said.

"Why not?" I said.

Melinda looked at me with some surprise. "You doing a lot of talking," she said.

"Yes, I am," I said. My dander was up, but I did not know why. "They got as many words in Spanish as they got in English."

"How come your mother lets you have the car?" Melinda said to the boy.

She was not taking time to get acquainted. You would think she'd relax and ask him some general questions. How have things been? Are you doing all right at school? A thousand questions like those. That is what I would have done if any grandchild of mine came by after a... a long absence, I guess you could call it. They had not quarreled. They just were not keeping in touch.

Of course, none of that would have happened with me. I am a regular Latin grandmother: the children come by on their birthdays and Easter and get their gifts. Then, of course, there is Christmas. That is a big to-do. I would not lose touch. True, I've got only one grandchild, Nellie; all the family genes are riding on her alone. I cannot afford to lose track of her.

Whereas Melinda's kids all have a minimum of four, which if you multiply by five, the number of children Melinda and Serfín had, gives you twenty. That is a lot of traffic. A couple of them could be lost in the shuffle and be well lost. That was dumb of me to say that—that's what happened with Sean's father, killed riding a motorbike. Still, Melinda always reminds me of those birds you see on television who push the babies out of the nest or off the teat and go off about their business without a look back.

"Which high school you go to?" I asked, trying to make the conversation more general.

"Jefferson," he said in a voice so flat you knew he did not want to hear another word about it.

"Well, that's that," Melinda said. She was no dummy. She looked at me as if to say, serves you right. "So what is your mother sending you over for?" she said.

"Nothing," he said.

"That's good," Melinda said, "because if there's something I can do without—it's a problem."

I said, "Melinda doesn't mean that."

"Isn't there something you want?" she said.

"I guess I will have that sandwich," he said, and spread his legs across the kitchen. "Yep, I'll do that."

Melinda began to take things out of the refrigerator and the cupboards. "I'll heat up a couple of slices of the pork," she said. "With a little of its own gravy."

Sean half straightened in his chair so that he could get his nose closer to the container with the slices of pork neatly layed out. They looked very inviting—taste even better, especially after the heat released all its flavors. I might as well come out with it—it would taste better when the heat let you smell the garlic. We Latins are masters at the use of garlic, and we should not be ashamed to admit it.

"Hmmmm," Sean said.

"You ever get down to Ybor City and get some Latin food?" she asked him.

"That's just a tourist trap," he said.

"I'm gonna heat it on top of the stove," Melinda said, and carefully lifted three slices on a spatula. "And this ain't no tourist trap."

I said, "I haven't had a pork sandwich in a long time."

She made a face at me, but she put in a couple more slices. "And see this bread?" she said to him, grabbing the morning's fresh Cuban loaf from the counter. "I'm gonna warm it, not toast it. You warm it, ya don't toast it."

"I can feel myself getting smarter by the minute," Sean said, and we all laughed.

"Tell me, I won't get mad," Melinda said to him. "Must be something you want—now or in the future—that made you come over. It doesn't mean you're selfish, it just means you're human. We want something, so we do something."

Sean looked skeptical. I don't mean he necessarily disagreed (though if he knew Melinda the way I knew her he would be mighty careful about disagreeing with her), that was not the point. The point was, would she really not hold it against him to have a reason that was not her reason?

The smell of the pork sandwich began to be wafted about the kitchen. I sat down to be ready for mine. Sean drew in his legs and I swear his nostrils flared a little. Melinda removed the four long pieces of bread—have you any idea of how light and savory Cuban bread is?—from the little broiler/oven and placed them on dishes. The two of us watched her lift the slices of pork and lay them on two slices of the bread and then place the top slices over them. She cut each sandwich in half and then passed a finger over the knife and licked at the bit of sauce she picked up.

"I tell you the truth, Grandma, what was in the back of my mind," Sean said. "I want to have something like this to do, whenever. Ordinary like. A place I can stop off going from here to there and see my grandma."

"Right!" Melinda said. She snapped her fingers and pointed at me before she placed the plates in front of us. "That's what I was saying to Sylvia when you interrupted us. Ordinary things. They really are important. Not the fighting and yelling and going up to bat."

She looked at him and at me as always—daring us to contradict her.

Who wanted to?

She leaned back on the kitchen counter and enjoyed the way we chewed the pork sandwiches. In a moment, she said, "I wonder why I was thinking about that?"

The Place I Was Born

I am sixty; my mother is eighty. I live in New York City; she lives in Tampa. Until last year she lived in the section called Ybor City where Spanish speaking cigar makers settled more than a century ago. She spent her entire life in the old house that my grandparents moved to from Key West. She never budged from Tampa—not even during the Depression when many cigar makers went North looking for jobs—and getting her out of the family house took my brother, Eddie, and me years. He lives in Boise and is a few years younger—four, I think. Mother was sixty-three when Father died, and that is when we first began to talk to her about moving: a good part of Eddie's and my lives were spent on the subject, when you think about it.

I used to take turns with Eddie (Mother calls him Edmundo) coming to Tampa every other year to keep up what we called our two-pronged campaign. He would report on his lack of success on the phone after each trip, and I would always end that conversation with: "I wouldn't listen to you either—anybody that moves to Boise from Tampa, man, you're a two-time loser!"

Now that she has finally sold the old house at what she thought was a fair price, he and I have come on a visit at the same time. A kind of celebration. (Our wives stay out of all this, particularly visiting Florida or one another or Mother.) Mother now lives with her sister, also a widow, in one of those apartment buildings for retirees sponsored by some Protestant denomination or the other, but the old house is as much on her mind as ever. Our first morning there and she wants to be taken to it, not the Centro Asturiano Cemetery where our father is buried.

She considered it some sort of negligence that the young, black couple did not think to stay home that day. Not that she had called them: Latins believe it is bad manners to give advance notice that you are coming by, as if you were asking them to go to the trouble of entertaining them. Before she left the car, she looked at the unmowed lawn and her lips became thin.

"If I had a daughter," she said after circling the house on foot and finding other faults, "every last room in this house would have been filled and I would not have sold it..."

"Forget about it, Mom," Eddie said. "Let's go eat one of those Cuban mixed sandwiches—there's nothing else in Tampa."

"Forget about it?" she said.

The house began as a shotgun house, but a third bedroom was added, then a little back room that in time was called the TV room, and finally a wrap-around porch. During the war, the shed became a carport with what is called a utility room attached. The yards in front and in back of our house were a tiny bit larger than the rest on the block, but not much more. When I was a kid there were sweet banana trees along the back fence; later, orange or grapefruit; finally, a camphor tree. In front, two palm trees always.

She had kept everything in the house too clean for its own good. She wore out tile and linoleums and paint jobs from washing them with strong soaps, not from use. The annuals and the perennials were urged mightily to grow and bloom. She fertilized and mulched. She watered and trimmed, and she fought the holly which she felt grew at too fast and wild a pace. The moment a frond of either of the palm trees out front began to wither, off it went. She did all this herself. No one, of course, had ever been hired to come in and clean; no was allowed either to mow the tiny lawn or to garden but she.

She also cooked and baked too much. All Spanish and Cuban dishes and desserts. And each time, of course, the oven had to be scrubbed clean. Eddie had bought her a dishwasher, but she did not trust it. Finally, she began to admit that washing down the big porch and its walls with scrub brush and hose was hard on her arthritic pains. Two years and a half ago, her sister was widowed, and she caved in: they would move in together. But neither would move into the other's house and that is how we got them to apply to the church-sponsored apartment building in the Hyde Park area. She was self-conscious about abandoning Ybor City for the good part of town where, as they used to say, the Americans lived, and did not tell many people about her move.

She called a realtor that a neighbor's relative had once used, and then the real struggle began. Whereas in the past it was Eddie and I who called her every other week or so, she now began to call us regularly to complain about the realtor, to make declarations about what she would do with the rooms full of furniture and linens and china, and to find fault with the people who came by to look at the house. Also, to question the motives of the younger cousins who now came by to visit her.

"I didn't like the way your cousin Yvonne was asking what I planned to do with the porch furniture," she once began a conversation, and ended up saying, "Everything is going to be for sale. I'm going to have one of those garage sales and pick up a penny or two. It's time I started thinking about myself."

That was during a call to me. Two days later, she called Eddie to tell him that she did not like the idea of a garage sale. It was mercenary and bothersome, she said. Eddie said she was not obliged to have a garage sale, and she hinted that I was expecting her to hold one instead of calling Goodwill and having them cart off everything.

"Anyway, I must give something or the other to each and every member of the family," she said. "I owe a lot of favors."

Eddie called me, and at first he seemed to believe that I had brought up the subject with her and urged the garage-sale solution on her. "Why would I?" I said to Eddie finally, and he came up with a laugh not an apology. That irked me.

"A garage sale would only prolong the agony," I said. "Think of all the phone calls about what to price each item!"

Mother had never been anything but straightforward and truthful in her ways, but we learned not to take any development in the sale of the old house at face value. Was the realtor as sneaky as she said? Did he practically force her to absorb closing costs for Damon Thigpen? Should she give Mrs. Thigpen the refrigerator and kitchen table and chairs as if it were part of the sale price?

"If I'm giving a gift," she said, "I'm giving a gift, not the realtor getting the credit for making it part of the sale price."

Eddie was on the whole laid-back about these matters, but I occasionally commented on her arguments, and it all eventually got reported to Eddie as *my* arguments.

"Part of the sale price?" I said to her. "People usually throw in the stove, but that's all."

Eddie called. "Why don't you let the old lady give them whatever she wants?" he began, and then laughed. "I fell for it! I fell for it! I owe you."

I reminded him of it that day when she stepped across the street to talk to Corona before going to La Tropicana. "You're paying for the sandwiches," I said. Corona had known us most of our lives, so we had to greet her, too. She said, "They are in trouble. Not from anything they have said directly to me, but from what I hear."

Corona had a way of sounding mysterious about non-Latins. She would not admit that although she had come to Ybor City from northern Spain when she was sixteen, she still did not, forty years later, speak English. She consequently reported their doings and their conversations with a great deal of indirection, so as not to give herself away.

"More trouble," Mother said. "Ah, me. Let us not discuss it anymore."

Corona did not spare her: "It would not surprise me if they are selling it."

On the way to La Tropicana, Mother enumerated the things she had done for the couple. The closing costs she had paid at the realtor's suggestion; but giving them the kitchen set and the porch furniture was her own idea. "I would have given them the hanging plants, too, except his wife hinted about them and no nice person does that."

In the parking lot of La Tropicana, Eddie said, "It's their house now, Mom—how they keep it is their business."

"You never had a drop of sentiment in you," she said.

She took time off from worrying about the fate of the house to point out that the ham in her sandwich had not been glazed. "Do you see that old-fashioned iron they used to glaze it with? They always kept it right behind the counter by the big hams. Like the iron my mother used on clothes. They're too busy serving all these crackers who don't know any better."

She believed it was the wife who neglected the house. She had never really cared about it. "I do not think she would like any house," Mother said, "but he was different. It does not have anything to do with their being Negroes."

I said, "Who said anything about that?"

"And the real Cuban mixed sandwiches do not have lettuce and tomatoes," she said. "You are taking me back to the house when we finish here."

Mr. Thigpen was sitting on the porch steps, his head in his hands, as if posing for a picture of dejection. Eddie and I had never met him, but he hardly had the energy to respond to our self-introduction. Mother had not done it; she was eager to get on to what interested her.

"You going to sell the house?" she said.

"I can't keep up the payments," he said.

"It looks terrible," she said. "Nobody will buy it the way it looks now."

"I'm just going to let the bank take it over," he said, sounding angry himself. "I already missed the payment last month."

Mother threw a hand up, the way she used to when she was impatient with Eddie or me.

"Your wife ought to go out and get a job," Mother said.

He must have had a lot of complicated feelings about his wife: he did not say anything, only looked away.

Mother turned her back on him and headed for our car.

Eddie actually said, "Good luck, Mr. Thigpen."

Mother decided to speak to Corona first. Thigpen went back to sitting on the steps. Corona in turn walked her over to our car.

Corona said, "They are not frugal like us."

Without saying anything to us, Mother crossed the street again. We saw her open her pocketbook and take out her wallet. Thigpen got up and shook his head. She stared at him and stopped counting bills from the wallet. She said something emphatic and shook her head and came back to us.

She said, "Come, it is time to go."

Corona stepped back and then waved as I drove off.

At the corner, Thigpen's wife turned into the block driving an old pickup truck. The kids were in back.

"Maybe if I talked to her..." Mother said.

This time I said, "Forget it."

Mother did not let us take the freeway which takes you to Hyde Park in five minutes. We no longer argued about it; I stayed on the old city streets and I have to admit you see more that way. I said that to Eddie and he added, "If you want to see more of this town."

We were barely out of Ybor City when Mother said, "I know what I will do—I will buy the house."

"No, you won't," Eddie said.

I said, "What makes you think the bank will sell it to you at a reasonable price."

I saw Eddie disagreed but kept himself from saying so.

"Turn around," she said. "I want to go to the bank and talk to them right now."

Eddie slowed down but kept heading west on Columbus.

"You buy that house and you won't have any money left for yourself," Eddie said, and accelerated without meaning to. "Tell her." He looked at me for support.

"How do you know?" Mother said to Eddie. "You do not know the state of my finances."

Eddie parked on a worrisome street. He said, "You don't have to go to the bank, you can buy it from him."

What the hell, it was the place I was born. I said, "We could buy it together. But you do not move back there."

"How do I explain it to my wife?" Eddie said.

"You talked her into marrying you," I said.

"I will leave it to you when I die," Mother said. "You can tell her it is a very good investment."

"You're never going to die," Eddie said, but he was already making a U-turn.

"You leave this to me," Mother said. "I will ask him what is a rental he can meet. And if it suits me, I will let him be the tenant. He knows he cannot fool around with me—one month he does not pay and he is evicted."

Eddie said, "I pity them," and I did not contradict him.

Still thinking ahead, Mother said, "Another day I'll show her how to wash down the porch and sides with the hose I gave them."

The Girls on the Block

Mama's paper bag became unstuck at the bottom, and a potato got away—at the very moment when she realized that the black girl at the bus stop was one of *them*. Aha. She had passed her earlier on the way to Angie's store and thought what funny skirts girls are wearing. And that's all. She'd heard plenty about them being only a block away on Nebraska Avenue, but had never seen one.

What was she going to do about the potato? Another one slid out, and two tomatoes and one pepper were in danger.

Mama brought her other arm around the bag and held on, the way she had hugged her belly during her first pregnancy. What must she look like? Her own mother used to laugh at her then. Out of the corner of her eye she saw that shiny, little, black skirt shaking up to her and creasing even smaller as the girl bent over and picked up the potatoes.

"It's leather!" Mama exclaimed, and the girl's face appeared at the level of her paper bag and said something like "Ooo-yaw."

Everything must be showing on the other side when she leaned over like that. A passing car honked. Mama straightened and looked stiff, insulted. Automatically, without thinking.

The girl said something unintelligible and flipped a hand with a disdainful motion of her wrist. Mama nodded her angry agreement, though she suspected the girl had used a bad word, and the car moved on.

The vegetables at the bottom were now secure, but the little package of Kleenexes fell out the top. The girl picked that up, too, and another car honked.

This time they laughed.

The girl said something that sounded less angry, and Mama said, "You said?" though she figured it was about the boys laughing in the car. Maybe a bad word again, for the girl shrugged and looked down, somewhat ashamed, Mama guessed, of what she'd called the boys, and then shook her head and laughed again.

Mama gaped at her: Her lips were thin and prettily shaped, her nose not what people expect. The girl said something that sounded mild and gave her body a wriggly shake. But Mama still didn't understand and she was going to ask if she was from up north, New York or Cleveland where two of her children lived, when the girl laughed once more and held up the potatoes in one hand and the Kleenexes in the other, like a girl in a TV commercial.

Then, miraculously, the words came through clearly. The girl said, "Ain't no car gonna offer me a ride with me like this." But Mama still gaped, and she became unintelligible again.

She wore a fuzzy, pink puffball of a sweater. No sleeves, but a sweater nevertheless. It brought Mama out of her trance. After all, it was Florida in May. "Aren't you hot in that?"

She looked Mama in the eye—a little mean, that look—and laughed an evil laugh.

Mama couldn't have explained why, but she laughed, too.

Immediately, the girl became understandable. "No way ya can carry that motern bag. Where ya goin?" Mama indicated her block across the street. "I'll carry the Kleenexes and the potatoes—wheee! Let 'em think I'm a homebody."

For the first time, Mama saw that the little, leather skirt didn't meet the sweater. No sir. That supple stretch was no belt but her flesh, and right in the middle where the buckle should have been, believe it or not, her navel.

Mama wanted to say no to be polite, the way Latins like her had been taught, but nodded twice because the girl might misunderstand. One, because she was black. Two, because she was—well, maybe she wasn't.

But, anyway, there was no stopping the girl. She said her name was Lula, led Mama across Nebraska faster than Mama had walked in a long time, then slowed down those long, shining black legs (did she oil them?) to stay in step with Mama and asked, "You be one of these Porto Ricans from down here?" All this just as Mama began to worry what the old women on her block would think, seeing them go by together.

Mama said, "No." It came out in a little gasp because, one, she wasn't Puerto Rican, and, two, she saw Melba raise her fat behind from her glider, her staring eyes round as marbles. "My mother was brought here from Spain when she was a baby, and my father came from Cuba."

Lula thought it over. "That make you Hispanic. You know, like TV when they tell you how many outta work. This many black, this many Hispanic?"

Mama still felt like objecting, but she had to nod. You could call her Hispanic; wasn't that funny.

Lula caught her hesitation and again said something unintelligible.

"You said?" Mama said, putting on a smile for the sake of Chela directly across the street from staring Melba. She was falling into her rose bushes, in a manner of speaking. She would be the first to tell her daughter, Vilma. It gave her a queasy feeling to think of Vilma now—50 and still a good, unmarried girl on her third vacation away from her, traveling with other decent single girls like her, this time to Hawaii. Even when Vilma was a teen-ager and they used to take her to Clearwater Beach, she hadn't displayed as much flesh swimming as Lula did waiting for a bus.

"Better'n a cracker," Lula said.

Mama laughed out loud at that and heard a screen door open on their side of the block. It was Alice, who never missed a thing, and she came down her porch steps and said, "Everything all right?"

Mama said, "Couldn't be better," and walked on.

Alice's sister, Graciela, watched from inside, cautious since the black boy came up to her porch asking for directions and reached out and yanked the gold chain from her neck. No more than she deserved for trying to find out whom he was visiting. The most exciting event of the year.

Her own daughter, Vilma, had said, "What can you expect—with all those girls on Nebraska!" Vilma didn't like those girls. Mama had named her after Vilma Banky, into whose tent Valentino had crept.

Could this Lula be one of those girls really? Mama looked at her oiled legs and that little skirt. Oh, there was no doubt, and she laughed again.

For the rest of the block, Lula didn't become unintelligible again. She told Mama about herself and began by saying she came from Boston. She waved a hand and almost lost a potato. "Thas a lie. I'm ashamed a Harlem."

"Such a famous place," Mama said.

"You heard somethin' good about it?" Lula said.

They laughed again and Lula said she had come to Florida to visit her grandmother. Her daddy's mother. He had shown up for the first time in years and that's how she found out just where in Florida she had a grandmother. "I gotta tell you I wished it was Miami. But I come to Tampa to try my luck anyway. In Harlem, even luck don't have a chance."

"She must be glad to see you," Mama said.

Lula gave a little shriek and followed Mama up the steps to her porch and became unintelligible again. She shook her head toward Nebraska and Mama heard the word "cousin" before her ears stopped functioning again. Mama was afraid Lula didn't like her cousin or her grandmother.

But Lula liked the plants on the porch. She grew some on the fire escape in Harlem. "When I was a kid. No more."

"It's no use here, too," Mama said. "They steal them off the porch at night. My daughter, Vilma, fusses with them. I don't bother."

"You got a daughter?" Lula said.

So it was Mama's turn, and she told her she had children and grandchildren up north and Vilma here living with her. "She never married," Mama said as if Lula had asked.

"I ain't never gonna marry," Lula said. "Never." She placed the potatoes on the porch table where Mama had unloaded her things, then slowly said, "Well," and went back to the steps and looked down the block to Nebraska like a condemned prisoner. "I betta go back and raise some money to go home."

She didn't look at Mama. It had just come out without her meaning it to.

Mama quickly asked her to have some lemonade. "You sit down awhile. I'm all alone. You can catch the next bus."

"Oh, yeah, there's always a next bus," Lula said, and gave her that sharp, mean look. "Okay, I sit," and she flopped down on a nylon-webbed aluminum chair.

The last thing Mama saw as she went inside was Lula sitting with her legs stretched out like a boy and the little, leather skirt had climbed up her thighs and disappeared. Rosario across the street no doubt could see, as they used to say, all the way to Port Tampa.

She hurried to the kitchen, found the tray Vilma insisted on using even when serving only a glass of water, and poured two glasses from the pitcher in the icebox. She could hear Vilma correct her: "Refrigerator, mother."

Poor Vilma.

Vilma liked to bring her lemonade when she sat out on the porch. Vilma liked to fuss. The whole block always knew when Vilma had brought her bad-tempered, old mother a glass of lemonade and the old woman hadn't appreciated it.

Poor Vilma.

Vilma never let her walk over to Angie's store, of course, and she would have taken all the groceries directly inside. Mama stopped, transfixed by a new thought, and forgot to close the refrigerator door. She had left her pocketbook out there, too. All the spending money Vilma had given her in new bills for the whole two weeks she was going to be away. She was being punished for her bad thoughts about Vilma. She must not run to the porch. That girl wouldn't take it.

Why shouldn't she?

It made her flesh crawl to hold herself back. She picked up the tray but she could not hold it steady. And she hadn't fixed a plate with the Social Tea cookies. The refrigerator door was open. She put down the tray. She took a deep breath. Was the money in the stupid Christmas wallet lying on top? She told herself to be calm and she did everything she had to do: the crackers on Vilma's pretty Spanish plate, extra ice in a soup bowl.

That black girl was a good girl. She only needed to get back to New York. Mama had some more money, money Vilma didn't know about. It was hidden under the linoleum in her bedroom. That was the way you saved money in the old days when banks folded before an ordinary person could tell. Mama prepared herself for the worst.

She opened the screen door and tried not to look at the pocketbook, but she must have because Lula immediately said, "You left your bag. I can see ya wallet. I shoulda taken it. Isn't that what we suppose to do?"

Mama didn't know what to say. Lula hadn't said a bad word and she'd heard her clearly: no static. So Mama settled for, "My goodness," and hoped Lula would not become unintelligible.

She did.

Mama pushed the pocketbook off the table and placed the tray in its place.

Lula said, "You mad with it or somethin'?"

Mama leaned over her and said in a low voice, "Lula, do you need some money?"

Static again, then Lula said, "Who doesn't?"

Mama said, "You're funny."

"Thas how white ladies test cleaning women, leave their money around. Like it's an exam."

Mama wished she could say that she didn't know that. She straightened and looked away and saw that there was some old fool or other out on every porch on the block. All on account of this girl. All looking her way, like bystanders on TV.

"And don't say my goodness," Lula said, "or I'll start in cussin'."

Lula gave her her mean look and Mama looked right back without wavering. This was it; take me or leave me. The mean look turned into a smile that showed her perfect, specially white teeth. "You passed my test, you know."

Mama said, "Now that's settled. How much money do you need to get back to Harlem?"

Lula took one of the dumb cookies. "You just like my mama. You don't mind your own business." But her beautiful teeth were still in view. "I'm gonna drink your lemonade and thas enough," she said slowly.

"Well, then, tell me all about yourself," Mama said, settling back, sure that Lula would never be unintelligible to her again, ever.

◇

Mama sat on the porch and watched Vilma go off with her dainty packages of souvenirs from Hawaii for all the old gossips on the block, and knew that she was in trouble. Which one would tell her? Rather, which one would tell her first? Your mother made friends with one of the girls on Nebraska Avenue. Pause. One of the black girls who wave at cars. One of *them*.

Vilma would surely not let on how she felt when she heard. She hadn't worked in the complaint department at Sears for twenty years to be caught off guard. No pursing of the lips; indeed, an interested yet not encouraging smile. But when she got home, it would be another matter.

Fat Melita, across the street and one house over, with her little gurgling laugh would tell Vilma. Clara next door was too near. Mama saw Clara try to inveigle Vilma inside out of earshot, but she failed. She said she wanted to show Vilma where she was going to place the little wooden pineapple souvenir, but had to settle for trailing after Vilma to fat Melita's porch.

The last words Mama heard clearly were Vilma's. "It's hand-carved," she said in the same tone she had been using with all of them since she was a child: precocious, unselfconsciously condescending. And as they had always done, they responded with a show of delight, enough delight to last Vilma a lifetime. Mama feared that now they laughed at Vilma behind her back and she didn't have the heart to tell her she sounded prissy. Vilma was fifty, she wasn't going to change.

Mama was seventy-one. She wished she could be spared all these fools on the block. Eleven of them. Private eyes, everyone. Vilma was distributing eleven of those damned pineapples. She was sure to listen to each one on the subject of the black girl and only smile and leave them frustrated, but she would repeat to her every word they said and add a few of her own and Mama would feel she was kept in after school.

Eleven of them, Mama's age more or less. Mostly widows, the rest with Latin husbands who took off immediately after dinner to the Spanish Club to play dominoes. The Latins in Tampa had been following that sort of routine for one hundred years, but now the block at evening was left entirely to old women: the children had moved away and the grandchildren showed up on Sundays. If you were lucky. Mama's two sons and their children lived in New York and Chicago.

She wished they were here right now.

There was Vilma, with Clara still trailing, coming back with her mouth set in a fake smile, a sure sign of extreme annoyance. A pose she had picked up at Sears, and it was no bargain.

Mama said something aloud in Spanish, a good language for cursing, and to her surprise someone answered. A little, old man on the sidewalk who'd approached from Eighth Street while she had been following Vilma's pilgrimage in the other direction.

He called her Leonora. He must go way back.

"Gabriel," she said, recognizing his thick eyebrows. "Gabriel Gomez, how are you?"

Vilma put aside her chagrin as if for a new customer, and recognized Gabriel easily, for she had been at his wife's funeral a month ago. Mama had not gone. Vilma was her emissary at such affairs.

Mama said, "Gabriel, you know how it is with me and..."

"I know, I don't blame you. Funerals aren't what they used to be."

Even Vilma enjoyed his saying that. Maybe she would forget what the private eyes had told her.

"What a surprise to see you on our block," Mama said.

Vilma said, "You've forsaken the Spanish Club?"

Gabriel was so happy to have two women speak to him that he was at a loss for a reply.

"Vilma, you were a little girl just the other day," he said, and added, when he realized he didn't sound gentlemanly, "And you're still as young as ever."

Mama said, "She was just in Hawaii for two weeks, on vacation."

Gabriel didn't know what to say to that.

He sighed. "Such a long time," he said; he meant since Mama's husband had died, his old partner at rabbit and quail hunts and fishing expeditions on the Gulf and at dominoes.

He remembered the excuse he had prepared. "I'm out for a walk."

Mama said quickly, "Come have your second coffee with us. I was waiting for Vilma before I made it."

Gabriel was so pleased that it immobilized him.

"Don't tell me you're one of those who believe the Americans when they say coffee isn't good for you."

"Never," Gabriel said. "Never."

Vilma decided which was the best chair for him and he sat in it stiffly but happily.

He announced, "My daughter wants me to move in with her."

"What a good idea," Vilma said.

"I'm not doing it," Gabriel said. "Too many children around there, no Latins, and she only makes instant coffee."

"Right you are," Mama said. "Hear that, Vilma?"

"Only in the morning when I'm in a hurry," Vilma said, and Mama went inside saying he would get no instant from her.

Mama looked at the backyard from the kitchen window, then got a tray and placed three demitasses on it and a sugar bowl. Before the coffee was ready she'd decided Gabriel had not just happened to walk by.

That Lula! She was making her worse than she already was. In her mind Mama saw the black girl smile a wicked smile.

Gabriel had come by on purpose.

That Lula put such thoughts in her head. Gabriel courting her? She slapped the counter top and laughed inaudibly. She wished she could tell Lula.

No, she must not encourage her with suggestive talk. Lula was on the verge of giving up her temporary profession. She must get her back home to New York. It sobered Mama to think of Lula's troubles. Come to Tampa to try her luck with a grandmother who didn't welcome her, and now she was stranded with no money.

She must have been wrong about Gabriel, she thought later. He drank his coffee, reminisced a little, and when one of Vilma's middle-aged girlfriends came to talk about the trip they had just made to the Pacific, he got up and left.

They were going to talk about that vacation until it came time to plan the next one. Six more months of Hawaii at least. Mama went inside to watch *Sixty Minutes*, got angry at all the injustices, and then went to bed before Vilma was done with her friend. Mama saw Vilma stand in the doorway of her bedroom and decide not to wake her to talk about what the eleven private eyes had told her.

In the morning Vilma's routine was too strictly timed to allow for talk, and, besides, this was going to be her first day back at work. More of those wooden pineapples for her friends at Sears. A reprieve. In the afternoon Vilma went straight into the bathroom for her shower. When she came out, she could smell her favorite meal cooking: liver and onions.

Mama knew from Vilma's smile that she saw through her. The hurricane would blow later.

After the first bite, Vilma said, "In Honolulu all the native dishes are very sweet."

Mama encouraged her on that subject. Yesterday Vilma had covered the scenic aspects.

Why should I be afraid because Lula comes by every midday for a glass of iced tea and a little talk?

Lula came from Harlem and that was a lot more interesting than Hawaii. So was soul food.

When there wasn't an onion or piece of liver left, Vilma looked up at Mama and said, "Mama, you haven't been listening and I know why."

Thank God, there was a knocking at the front door. Mama standing, about to make coffee, and Vilma sitting at the end of the kitchen table could both see through the living room and make out clearly the figure outlined in the screen door.

"Who's that?" Vilma said, but she knew.

"Lula!" Mama said, and hurried past Vilma. "What's the matter?"

"You here, that's good!" She flattened herself against the screen door, holding one hand to the side of her face and looked back into the street. "I'm in trouble, trouble. Can I come in?"

Then she saw Vilma.

"Oh-ooh, I forgot," she said, and looked at the space between Mama and Vilma. "How you?"

"Come in, come in," Mama said. Vilma be damned.

Lula slipped inside. She shivered. “Mama, it’s my cousin. You know.” She looked at Vilma. “The one bring me over to Nebraska every day?”

“I know,” Mama said. She reached up and took Lula’s hand away from her face. “Oh, oh.” And she cursed.

“Don’t take on now, don’t take on.” Lula covered the bruise again. “You warned me. He caught on I put money aside from each—you know—so’s I could get my fare back to New York.”

Vilma gasped.

“I’m sorry,” Lula said. “No offense.”

That’s the way she talks to white people, Mama thought.

“Never mind,” Mama said. “Where is he? I’ll get the police—”

Lula turned away quick. She opened the screen door.

Mama pulled her back. “What’s the matter with me. Of course, I won’t call no police.”

Lula cursed under her breath.

“Go on, tell me,” Mama said.

“He’s out there looking for me, Mama. I cut through one of your neighbor’s backyard.”

“Oh, my goodness,” Vilma said. She tucked away the observation that the girl called Mama, Mama.

Mama put the latch on the screen door and stepped back to close the inner one. There was a man on the sidewalk. She almost screamed. Then she laughed. It was Gabriel.

Gabriel tried to walk so slow he was shuffling. Then he stopped and stared.

Mama opened the door. "Gabriel, come up and have coffee." She motioned to Lula and Vilma. "I'm sitting on the porch with him—you stay inside."

All eleven private eyes were out on their porches, too. Gabriel didn't notice, but Mama was so busy keeping watch, looking for Lula's cousin, that tramp, that she couldn't think of a word to make conversation.

"Well," she finally said. "You came at the right moment." She raised her voice. "Vilma was just going to make coffee. Vilma!"

Vilma stuck her head out the door. "Hello, Gabriel, how are you, I'll be with you soon." And disappeared.

Gabriel didn't notice anything strange about that. He was struggling with his opening statement. Finally, he got it out. "My daughter is right, the house is too big for me."

Mama thought: how do I know he's her cousin, that pimp—aiee, aiee—who sets her on Nebraska every day? Maybe he's a professional criminal.

"We made such a good foursome in our day," Gabriel said.

Of course he was a professional criminal. She looked up the block, not at the porches—she knew what was there—but at the sidewalks. Time was, the great oak trees would not have let her see. No one coming from there.

"Your Ramon and me both from the same province in Spain. You and my wife both West Tampa girls.

Remember when we all rolled cigars at the same factory—Perfecto Garcia's?"

Over her shoulder she saw the movement. He turned the corner hurriedly from Eighth Street, long legs striding. He was black; you couldn't mistake him for Gabriel—ha-ha—the setting sun made his face shine, a live, wide-eyed look on it—darting more quickly than her own.

"And then Ramon had to go and die so young."

"Yes," Mama said, surprised she could get one word out.

He walked by, making himself slow down. A panther. The skintight tee shirt bisected between the pectorals by a rivulet of sweat. He gave their porch but a glance. Nothing there. Between his shoulder blades another clinging wet streak. The thoughts he made you think.

Maybe if she talked to him? Oh, no.

He gave Clara next door a look that cut like a knife. Abruptly he crossed the street towards fat Melita's. She stood at the veranda on her porch and Mama heard him calling out a question to her. Melita took a deep breath.

Behind the screen door Vilma gasped.

Mama stood. She kept her eyes on fat Melita. Lula's cousin repeated his question. Melita swallowed and said, "No." She shook her head for emphasis. "No."

Good Melita.

Mama sat down. Gabriel had talked through it all. He still had that funny look. He waited for her to reply but didn't look her way.

"So what do you say?" he asked. "Do we join forces?"

Mama laughed, as much with relief as with comprehension.

"It is funny, you're right," he said. "But don't you think my solution has some merit?"

"Yes," Mama said, "if we had an extra bedroom and there weren't eleven private detectives living on this block watching my every move."

"As a boarder?" he said. "I didn't mean—"

"You couldn't have meant anything else, Gabriel," Mama said. "The last romantic thing I did was name my daughter Vilma. And that was a long time ago, I've lost the knack."

"You were always outspoken and to the point; I like that." But he was disappointed.

Mama heard the murmurings behind the screen door. "Wait," she said to Gabriel, got up and opened it part way and talked to them half in, half out.

"Lula is staying here and later we'll figure out how much money she needs to get back to New York."

Vilma said, "We have already come to that conclusion. No one needs your advice."

Lula said, "She just like you."

"Go put a cold towel on your face," Mama said. "And Vilma, where's the coffee?"

"I heard that fool out there," Vilma said. "Men think we want them in our bed, all of them. I'm glad you let him know we can take them or leave them."

"Isn't that the truth!" Lula said.

"The things they don't know," Mama said. She took a quick look at Lula and saw she didn't mean it either.

They were both lying, but at fifty Vilma was still a good girl and had to be protected from the truth.

She went back to Gabriel. "I'll make you a counter-proposal. You can come by every evening and have your coffee with us. No one should drink coffee alone."

"Very well, I might as well stay now," he said, "and get something out of this visit."

Celia's Family

Celia heard the phone begin ringing before she opened the door to her small apartment in the Tampa Episcopalian Bayshore House. Lydia, she announced to the empty living room. She took time to put down the basket of folded, clean clothes on the sofa and to sigh deeply. Only then, as if fortified, she picked up the phone.

Lydia said, "Where were you? I called two times—"

"I don't know," Celia said. "Maybe I was downstairs doing the laundry—"

"Well, I called and called," Lydia said, "and there wasn't any answer every time."

"Okay," Celia conceded, but sounded critical.

No reply from Lydia. That was a plus. Lydia got it. She wasn't dumb; she knew she was being snubbed. At times like this—and Lydia called every morning and evening—Celia swore she could hear her cousin thinking during the pauses: casting about for something to ask, hoping for news, imagining there was some activity planned or going on from which she was being excluded.

And, of course, there always was: there were too many cousins in their family for Lydia to be up-to-date on their doings. Twenty-one first cousins, to be exact. And they had forty-nine children, none of whom were Celia's and all of whom consequently were like close nieces and nephews to her.

"Anything happened?" Lydia asked, as if that were her reason for calling. "I haven't heard from anybody."

"You didn't hear Bush lost?" Celia said. "Thank God."

"I didn't mean that," Lydia said quickly. "I knew that happened."

"You wouldn't hear it from those Cuban refugees of yours," Celia said. "They are probably in mourning."

"They do not talk about politics," Lydia said, waited a moment, and then added, "very much."

Celia sighed. "Is that so?"

"Not to me," Lydia said. "Not to me."

Celia sighed again. "You called to talk about them?"

"Me?" Lydia said. "Me!"

"Calm down, Lydia," Celia said.

"They live across the street," Lydia said. "I cannot do something about that."

"Please," Celia said.

With an intake of breath, Lydia got to the point. "Are you and Lola going out to the Tropicana?"

Celia recognized her gasp for what it was—intrepidity—and tried to throw her off—or, at least, make her work harder for an answer. She said, "Today?"

"I think so," Lydia said. "From something she said I figured it must be today."

"You were talking to Lola today?"

Lydia confessed, "Yes. She happened to call."

Celia said, "She called you?"

"I think so," Lydia said. "Maybe I did. I don't stand on ceremony."

Celia said, "Then why didn't you ask her?"

"You know how Lola is...you wouldn't think she is a sister, sometimes. You and I are cousins, but you are more of a sister than her."

"If Lola and I are going to have a Cuban sandwich at La Tropicana, she ought to know about it," Celia said. She waited. "At least as much as me."

"I have not had a good mixed sandwich in—in, at least, a month," Lydia said. "That's how long. I have no way of getting over to La Tropicana. Or anywhere."

"It's only a week since your car got dented," Celia said. "To hear you talk, people would think you are in a wheelchair."

"More," Lydia said.

"More?"

"That's how long the car has been with the body man," Lydia said. "It was another week before that when the boy hit me in the Tampa Bay Mall."

"Two weeks," Celia said.

"Two weeks?"

Celia said, "One week and one week makes two weeks."

"In my situation—I can't stand it—it seems like forever," Lydia said. She sighed but sounded angry rather than poignant. "It's not like living in your building. All those nice ladies on every floor, you always have company."

Celia could say a lot about that, but decided not to. They had had that conversation before, too.

"Or you can go down to the lobby. There is always somebody there. Or go to the hobby room."

"Don't play on my sympathies," Celia said. "Just come right out and say it: Take me to the Tropicana with you, poor little me."

"Why do you always have to put things that way?" Lydia said. "We weren't taught—"

"What way? What way?"

"So rough," Lydia said. "You wouldn't know we were brought up together. Your mother—she was as good as my mama, too, remember—she would not like it one bit. She was sweet."

"Mama always told the truth," Celia said. "Right out. And she wouldn't be friends with no Cuban refugees. They're not refugees, they're counter-revolutionaries."

"They are not friends, they are neighbors—"

"It doesn't sound like that to me."

"I come out the door and they are there. What am I to do? Front door, back door, it doesn't matter. Friends!"

"What do you want?"

"There, there! That's what I mean. You are so rough." There was a little squeak at the other end which meant Lydia was working herself up to a sob.

Celia waited a moment, but it was no use. She placed a hand over the phone and said a bad word.

"Celia, Celia!" Lydia called. "Are you there?"

Celia made a noise.

"Celia, are you gonna pick me up?" Lydia said. "Will you tell Lola I'm coming? Maybe you don't have to tell her. Why should you? We're all family. Just pick me up. You are so good."

"I'll call you back," Celia said. "Nothing was definite. Just be ready."

"I am ready, I am always ready," Lydia said. "I'll sit on the porch and wait for you. You are the only good one in the family."

"I'll call you first," Celia said. "Maybe nothing will happen. I don't know."

◊

Celia began with Lola by saying Lydia had called, and Lola immediately screamed.

"I haven't slept all night!" Lola said. "It's her doing and I'm sure she slept like the angel she is not."

"What? What?" Celia said, and began to laugh; that was Lola's gift, laughter.

"She called Leslie!" Lola said. "Would you believe it?"

"In Miami?"

"She reported me to my own daughter!" Lola said. "She told Lola that I treat her very mean."

"She told Leslie—"

"My own daughter. And Leslie believed her. Think of that. Leslie believed her. Would you believe it?"

Celia said, "I believe it," and felt much better.

She added, "Lydia can put on an act. I tell everyone in our family when she makes trouble, but I don't think I have convinced..."

"I didn't sleep all night," Lola said. "I didn't convince Leslie either. On both counts—I didn't convince her it was treachery for Lydia to call her, and I didn't convince her I was not mean."

Celia laughed.

"You want to hear all the things I thought up last night? First, I thought I would shoot Lydia dead," Lola said. "Get Cuco's old gun, which must be all rusty now, and shoot her there in her yard among all the weeds."

The image of Lydia's unmowed yard—all the cousins deplored it—made Celia laugh louder.

"Second, shoot Leslie, too."

And again Celia laughed.

"Don't laugh too much," Lola said. "She is my daughter, after all. Even if she is dumb."

That last was true, but of course she would never have said so.

"It's about time that old gun got used," Lola said. "Poor Cuco, may he rest in peace. Always worrying about burglars and he never got to use it, thank God."

"What did she tell Leslie?" Celia said, not wishing to comment on Cuco either. As she had told herself many a time, Lola has really needed her sense of humor.

"That I am mean to her, that I have no sisterly feelings, that I didn't take her to the Westshore Mall—that was last week when I yelled at her—though she is the oldest and deserving of much respect. Oh, God, what else? Also about last Sunday—I didn't pick her up and take her to that Protestant church she goes to, like a fool. I shouldn't say that."

"She knows better than to ask me to take her to any church," Celia said. "She is always feeling sorry for herself. But she doesn't stop a moment; she is always out."

"And she watches the soap operas too much," Lola said. "That's what I think."

Celia added, "And it's ridiculous for her to be going to a Protestant church at her age—I don't know what's happened to people."

Lola interrupted. "No, I tell you what it is. She went over to live with your family when mama went to the TB sanitarium and she stayed on and then married, so after she was ten she never lived with us. Of course, I don't feel as close to her as my other sisters."

Lola laughed after a pause. "That's not true," she said. "I feel closer to you and we never lived under the same roof."

Celia said, "She's just a pain, let's face it."

"Poor thing," Lola said, and laughed again.

"I guess I better pick her up then," Celia said.

"Oh, God, would you?" Lola said. "I'll meet you at La Tropicana. If I pick her up, I am going to get into a fight despite all my resolutions. This way it will be in public and I can act like a lady."

"That's okay," Celia said.

"I decided I wouldn't say a word to her. I decided this after a whole night of thinking, while I was having my café con leche this morning. Rise above it. Be a lady."

Celia laughed.

"You know, like American women. Upper class not white trash. You know what I'm saying—Latins don't rise above anything. We're in there swinging all the time. I embarrass myself whenever—"

"You don't mean that," Celia said. "Our mothers—"

"Your mother, not mine," Lola said, and laughed and laughed. "My mother was always yelling she had too many kids. And she cursed."

"The things you say, Lola," Celia said, and forgave Lola for going to all those fashion shows at ten dollars a head just to socialize and gossip and for lunching with her silly friends as if they were all still in high school. "Your mother suffered a lot."

"Poor thing," Lola said. "But not another word or I'll ruin my mascara."

That had become a signal for laughter with them, although Lola did wear mascara and it was unthinkable that Celia should.

"Though I have to tell you," Lola continued, "that it's a good thing to curse. It's better than an aspirin. I do it all the time when I am alone and there's nobody to hear me. I got into the habit with Cuco; he didn't like women to talk like men."

Celia murmured, "Yes, yes," although she had heard Lola confess this often.

"Celia?" Lola said in a small voice. "It was me who called Lydia, after all. I let her get to me; I didn't act like a lady. I can't lie to you."

"She said you called her," Celia said, "and that's how she figured out we were going to La Tropicana."

"La Tropicana? I didn't say a word about La Tropicana. I said a lot of things about her, but not a word about La Tropicana." Lola screamed again. "I said I was going to shoot her if she ever called Leslie again."

"No, you're not," Celia said. "Nobody's ever going to shoot Lydia. Not you or me. In fact, we are going to take her to La Tropicana and God knows where else, want to bet?"

Still gurgling with laughter, Lola said, "You know that old expression the men had—you're going to be wearing your ass in a sling? That's what I said. I don't know how it came to me; I haven't heard it in years. I was going to tell you all about it at lunch."

Celia said, "The lunch is ruined."

"I'm going to eat all my dessert," Lola said. "That will frustrate her. And don't you leave anything on your plate either. Let her starve."

"It's curious," Celia said. "She never said a word to me that you had scolded her. She told me you had called her and I didn't believe her. I thought it was the other way round."

"I call her sometimes," Lola said, and fell quiet.

Neither said anything for a moment.

Celia said, "I don't see how you can stand to have lunch with her. Today, anyway. You want me to call it off?"

Almost simultaneously, Lola said, "You know what it is, don't you—she doesn't want to die alone."

"She'll never die; she'll bury us both."

Lola said, "She is eighty-four."

"Eighty-four?" And Celia could see Lola at the other end nodding in her pitying way.

Lola said, "Poor thing."

Celia said, "She always wins."

"I'm calm now," Lola said. "It's always so good for me to talk to you—I don't have any sense. You're the sensible one in the family."

"Oh, I don't have any sense either," Celia said, but she accepted the compliment—another of Lola's gifts.

She then said, "I'll call Lydia and tell her to wait for me. If I can reach her—she's probably across the street being chummy with those refugees."

"Everyone talks to them now, Celia," Lola said. "You know, no one thinks about all that anymore."

Yes, but not she.

◇

Celia sat down on the sofa after speaking to Lola, meaning to achieve some sort of calm herself before calling Lydia to say she would come by at twelve-thirty. Before she got comfortable, it occurred to her that she was the loser in all this: it was more out of the way for her than for Lola to pick up Lydia, and she would undoubtedly end up paying the whole bill at La Tropicana. Never mind why that's so, she said aloud to the wall across the room with all the family pictures she had so carefully framed over the years—uncles and aunts, parents and grandparents, and all the people of her generation and the next. It's too complicated to explain, she added, just take my word for it. If Lola has one fault of character, it's that she's tight.

Yes, tight, and she got up to shake off the thought. It was not a nice one.

She stopped a moment in the middle of the room and looked out the picture window. The undulating shore of the bay stretched out ahead towards Ballast Point. All through her childhood in Ybor City, the Latino section of town—even until four years ago when she moved in here—she had always seen the bayshore from the window of a car. With wonder and awe as a child.

With feelings of social inferiority as she grew older. With acceptance, finally, that the bayshore was where the rich live and not she.

And yet here I am, she said to the picture window, living on social security, and then turned back to the phone, ready now to call Lydia. After all, she said, and never finished the thought. The phone rang as she stretched her hand towards it. Oh, she said, startled, Oh, and it was a moment before she got it to her ear. Her cousin Elvira's voice was already in the middle of a greeting.

"Hello, hello," she replied happily: it was a good sign that Elvira was able to call.

Elvira said, "Who is this?" She sounded stern, but Celia knew better.

"This is Celia," she said. "It's good to hear from you, Elvira dear, I was meaning to call myself."

"Celia?"

"Yes?"

Celia did not know, at moments like this, whether to wait and let the wheels of memory click into place for Elvira—or to rush ahead with talk and make it easier for her.

She rushed ahead with talk. "The reason I was going to call is that next time we should do something, not just sit in your patio. I was thinking it would be nice if I came by and took you off to La Tropicana."

She waited for only a second when Elvira did not reply.

"Remember how we cousins used to get together and eat Cuban sandwiches until we burst? I ate as much as the boys. Now, I can hardly eat a whole one."

She waited a little longer for Elvira this time.

"How times goes by. No one lives in Ybor City anymore," she finally said to fill the void.

In a thin voice Elvira said, "Ybor City?"

Celia laughed a false laugh. "Where all the Latinos and the cigar factories were neck and neck. I mean, no one in our family lives there anymore, do you realize that? You can't tell us from regular crackers."

She laughed again and again, but it sounded false, and she did not hear her cousin hang up.

"Elvira?" she said. "Elvira, I got an idea—why don't I come right now and pick you up and we'll—"

Elvira, she said to the picture window when she was sure Elvira was no longer listening. I did something wrong. Why did I say, Do you realize that... It was the wrong thing to say to one in her condition. Elvira is too sweet to hang up on me.

She also should not have said that about time passing by. She should have been smarter than that, been more thoughtful. Time was disappearing for Elvira.

And her time with Elvira was also disappearing, along with everything else in Elvira's mind. She stood in the middle of the room and swayed a little, feeling insubstantial. This evanescence was worse than death. Worse than her husband's death. With death, things ended, came to a stop, but they were there, they did not disappear. It was history, you referred to them, you said *May he rest in peace*, as he did about Julio every time she mentioned his name.

She held the phone to her ear for a long while, but Elvira had, indeed, disappeared. She placed the phone back on its cradle carefully, and walked over to the wall of photographs. Elvira was there—she and Elvira at age four sitting on the swing at Elvira's home on Ybor Street. They used to fly back and forth on it, madly pushing on the floor simultaneously on the downswing. *Let it rain, let it rain*! they sang in Spanish with shrill abandon, *The Virgin's in the cave*!

One rainy Saturday, on Lydia's first payday at the factory, they were shrieking on the swing and Lydia showed up and gave them a quarter each. A quarter!

What a terrible person I am, Celia said aloud. She walked with energy to the phone and rang Lydia. After three rings, she lost her eagerness to reach her and began to think that she had long ago repaid that quarter. She did not count the number of times she let Lydia's phone ring. She gave her enough time to walk in from the porch. Enough time to get home from the Cuban refugees, if the truth be told.

When she put the phone down, it rang immediately. It was Lola. She had thought it over and she hoped that Celia could come pick her up after she had picked up Lydia. "I don't trust myself to drive today," she said. "I'll sit in back and it won't be necessary to say anything and have a fight."

"Sure, sweetheart," Celia said. "I just called her and she was not there. If she's not on the porch when I come by, I won't wait. I'll just go on over to your house."

"Maybe I should call her?" Lola said.

"No, no, don't bother, she's given you enough trouble for one day," Celia said. "Life shouldn't be so complicated."

"Yes, let's hope she's not there and we can have a simple good time like we planned," Lola said, and laughed her infectious laugh. "Right?"

"Right," Celia said lightheartedly. She even laughed the laugh Lola always inspired, but as soon as she hung up and was left with her own self, she began to doubt. Now, she would be picking up both of them at each one's home and doing all the driving and paying for the whole lunch.

She looked at the wall of the family photographs and said, Being good doesn't come easy to me, and walked inside determinedly to select a cheery blouse to wear to lunch.

The Gardens of Long Island

I had learned to be brisk. Get to the point. It is a fact that drunks have to hit bottom to reform. The how-to books said so, my current friends too, finally the marriage counselor we went to said it in a session apart with me. It had got to look more and more that Lex was always going to be on the brink. Never a falling-down drunk. As it was, no one noticed he was a lush, even people whose bottles he emptied: like me they thought they were suffering from double vision or some momentary memory lapse. So no more hemming and hawing—I did it, I threw him out. On a Sunday evening: I wanted to start the week clean. So, clear the decks, everybody!

I picked up that kind of language from Lex who, got it from his Erie Canal enterprising Yankee ancestors. Ensconced amongst his ancestors was Admiral Perry. Or was it Dewey? I prefer to think it was Dewey, that rotten imperialist, and actually I hate his and his family's ho-ho-ho bully-boy language.

That Sunday night, our daughter Katrina (fourteen) was staying over at a friend's home, our son Damon (eight) was long ago fast asleep, the right time to tell Lex to pack up and leave. He was drunk, but he reacted well, as well as he always performed his job, no matter how tanked, when God knows he should not have been able to tell an azalea from a horse chestnut. (He was a gardener—excuse me, a landscape architect.) He looked at me for a long moment, then nodded and left. There was nothing he really had to return to the house for; all his books and drawing materials were at his super-neat office on Main Street. I even gave him the receipt for his shirts at the cleaners, and that was that. I didn't sleep all night, wondering where he was staying.

He did come back, of course. The very next day, after the kids had left for school. Maybe he thought I could not hold out. But it was he who wanted back, and he was ready to beg.

That was good for my ego, but it pushed him over the edge. He cried. That must have been hard on him, he was so macho. But then that was probably the ultimate in his campaign to win me over: a macho crying, that's real desperation. Still, I wish he had not done it.

I lost some of my feeling for him when I realized those beads running down his beard were tears. He went through his father's funeral without crying and so I did not recognize them for what they were. How did his beard get wet? I asked myself, feeling foolish at being distracted from my objective—to reform him. Tears!

I told him I was waiting for proof that he was through with alcohol.

He said, "Pussy, I am going to my first AA meeting tomorrow night. I would go tonight, but they don't meet until tomorrow. And I'm going to my first meeting with the Hamiltons tonight."

That shook me a little from my resolve, but I said nothing. "So?" I said, as if tapping my foot.

Truthfully, I wish I could have asked if the Hamiltons really meant that talk about commissioning him to design and plant a real maze, but it would have played right into his hands. From now on I was going to become uninvolved in his doings. Gardening, that's all it was, although he talked about it as if it were a new religion, and of course in the Hamptons they give a yardman's work fancy names. Landscape architect! I swear he had used up all the gardens of Long Island to deflect me from my purpose for three years now.

The research he did, the old books he hunted down in country bookstores—I went through it all with him. He sat down at night with the books and poured over them ostentatiously in the living room, a virtuous glass of iced water at his elbow. "Listen, Pussy," he would say at intervals and repeat an absurd bit of knowledge about French versus English gardens. Or "Listen to this, Pussy. The country people, it says, played spring games in the maze and many a summer's evening they knelt at the center to hear the fairies sing." He would exhale with the wonder of it. At first, I went along with him ardently, then I merely made encouraging noises, but always he would take a trip to the kitchen for what I called his solid liquids.

He thought his work was more important to everybody than their own lives.

"That's what she said I had to do, remember?" he explained beseechingly now, and wiped his beard on his sleeve as if it were sweat.

In a way it was: perspiration of the soul.

"She" was Deborah Alter, our marriage counselor.

Actually, she felt more like my marriage counselor than his, and perhaps that is the explanation for my mistakes. I tend to look for psychological explanations to things, so I felt closer to her: we were marching in step. Not that Lex didn't use her arguments to back up his arguments or rationale or whatever, but he mostly leans, when I think back on it, on whatever is at hand.

"She says I'm trying too hard to not shift the pressures on to you, that I'm being over-protective," he'd say and then study me to see if I bought it. "Instead, I take a drink too many...you know."

But why am I going over all this? What's done is done. Go on to the next thing. That may not be the Latino thing to do, but I stopped doing the Latino woman bit a long time ago. Not that I ever was much of one. I had a Puerto Rican grandfather and my mother named me Maria so I would not forget what was later called my ethnic background. I was also one-fourth Irish, one-fourth Scotch, one-fourth from one of those middle European countries where people have banged-up noses: either long and pointy and squashed at the end or broken up like a prizefighter's with a ledge above the nostrils. (I inherited this second variation and it has been a trial to me.) There was a period there, when we were all being different in the Sixties, that I wrote my name with an accent mark—María. I've dropped that, too. The feminists taught me that Latino women put up with more machismo than my other ancestors. So, let's face it, I'm just an American now, nose and all.

Lex was a Wasp through and through. Right back to Genesis, it sometimes seemed. He's got a straight, strong nose, and it flares threateningly during sex. We met in the Sixties—my mother said that in her generation we never would have even passed one another on the same street—and we did our thing and now the chickens are coming home to roost.

In that soft insinuating voice Lex said, "Pussy, do you want me to shave off my beard?"

That remark was a sexual innuendo that only I could explain, but I am not going into it. It is going to stay unexplained. I was in my own house, but I turned away and went straight to the car and went weekend shopping at the supermarket in Sag Harbor. Anyway, I was tired of sex and all that. He could let himself out; he still had the keys. But one of the kids told me when I got back that they found him in the living room when they returned from the movies. He was watching television.

"In the daytime!" I muttered without thinking.

Damon, who was always defending him, explained, as if I were a child, "It was a program about that court in England with the gardens." He looked at me as if I were responsible for his forgetting the name Hampton Court and the word maze.

Katrina just went on upstairs. She was in full retreat from us or, as they say now, in denial. Not a word to me, but there was nothing unusual that; I often could not remember what her voice was like.

I am going to have to explain about Lex and mazes and all that. Maybe if I talk about it, I'll understand it.

"On public television," Damon added. "It wasn't MTV."

I didn't answer, so he prodded me once more. "You hear about the maze?" he said, happy with himself that he had thought of the word and was one up on me about Lex.

That made me think. Did he know about us? Kids pick up on the slightest change in response. He added, "The Hamiltons are definitely going ahead with it."

I would have liked to know if they were giving him half or one-quarter acre to play with, but I was not going to ask Damon. I was through with garden talk—box versus yews, turf mazed for play versus formal ones for retreats and contemplation and hanky-panky.

I ran into Lex in Southhampton two days later. I did not get close enough to smell his breath, but his breath never had smelled the way the books say. I was on my way to my last session with Deborah Alter and I forgot about the Hamiltons and their formal garden in my hurry to get away from him. "I went to the group meeting," he said (he meant Alcoholics Anonymous but he could not bring himself to say it aloud outside the house), and I nodded and walked away. "Pussy?" he called after me.

I told Alter that I had done what I had to do and would not see her again unless I got into trouble. I agreed with her—she had gone so far as to volunteer that therapy wasn't very successful with alcoholics and recommended AA—but I did not like her. "Right?" I said.

She nodded, but that slight inclination of her head did not convince me she was replying.

"Right?" I said again.

She did not nod this time nor answer my question directly or indirectly—or in any way. I guess therapy is essentially hemming and hawing. Instead, she said, "You know about the AA?"

"He told you?" I said. "Me, I'm waiting for results."

"There won't be any," she said. "He joined a group composed of people already on the mend."

"What did I tell you about him," I said, and did not put it as a question. I should have told her he probably would come round at night for the old high jinks, but if I started in on that with her, I would probably end up the villain in everyone's mind.

Lex was supposed to meet with people who were at his stage of the game—drunks trying to get out of the gutter, as it were. That's how the AA works: you get help from buddies in the same mess as you, people you can't fool as he did me.

Deborah Alter started to tell me this once more—therapists either don't respond or they repeat things again and again—but I acted as if she had no more to say, which she really didn't. I got up and said goodbye. I meant it. I never went back to her.

I kept my distance from him, too, but I stayed in the Hamptons. No energy to make one more move, that's the reason, and in the Hamptons the kids could be near him. Anyway, I could not go back to anywhere in any sense. If only I could go back to the South Bronx or Israel or County Cork. That's the way it is nowadays—go back to your roots—but my mother is dead and I would feel like a fake making claims to any sort of ethnicity.

Why am I telling all this as if it happened yesterday? It did not. It happened almost ten years ago. Even the Republican era is over. Yet in all important ways nothing has changed, and both Lex and I have remained on Long Island, as has the depression or recession or whatever it is. But the expensive shops and the anxious high living still go on. And it's one place where people who adore mazes do not have to cut back on essential expenses like that. They say the rentals (which we all deplore, right?) are up again for the coming summer.

Some things, of course, did happen when I threw Lex out, and that's the problem. Our best friends, who had been living in Bucks County (after we all left Vermont, for one reason or the other: I cannot really recall why we originally settled down in Vermont, we thought then forever—oh yes, subsistence living), are here in the Hamptons, too. Dino and Cookie came to rescue us when I did not relent, and they stayed, like those would-be lifesavers who plunge into the surf and are dragged down by the people they had hoped to save.

This is what happened: Cookie jumped into bed with Lex the moment the coast was clear, and married him as soon as all four of us were out of the divorce lawyers' offices. That needs further explaining. When they came down with their two kids, they decided to move in with Lex—he had rented a rambling old house in Sunshine for its big grounds—because obviously it was Lex who was in bad shape. But they saw me a lot, too. Dino suddenly got a chance to take over the art workshop in an upstate college, which was just as good, I thought, because he only sat around and studied me with that abnormal stare of his. (Painters are always looking and not much else.) Since the appointment was only for one term, it seemed best to everyone (they even asked me and I agreed) that Cookie stay behind and work in Lex's gardening business.

Cookie and Dino were supposed to be conspiring with me to get him, as Lex used to put it, off the sauce and back home with me. Comes the second act: Katrina, while staying over with them one night, got up with a stomach ache in the middle of the night and went to the only parent around in that house and found Cookie in Lex's bed.

It was Dino, after all, who was the hardest hit of the four of us, but he is a figurative painter (which accounts for his intense way of staring at people) and figurative painting began to be acceptable again in this mecca of abstract expressionism, thank God. Good for his soul and career. He started to sell and a gallery took him on. You don't walk away from that sort of break when the only alternative is teaching in some Pennsylvania community college. He even tried to make it with me, but I began to laugh when he made the first overture and I couldn't stop. Maybe it's because he was rusty at it, but it ruined everything, like a sneezing fit.

Not that I was interested in sex with anybody.

"Dino," I said, to make it right between us, "what would be the difference? We know each other too well."

He laughed. "White man, I'm not circumcised!"

No romance. Never again.

Still, pretty dramatic, how we shifted around, you've got to admit, if you take the long view. From 1968 on, that is. I told Dino this once, and he shook his head and said we were just two nuclear families breaking up, not venturesome Sixties' hippies. He was right: it did not seem a drama when it was all unfolding, as we say in the business: it was all very Southern California then, very laid back. The "business" I refer to is soap opera—they bought my first script a year ago when their regular writers were on strike—but that's a sub-plot. It's me and Lex that is still the main story line. I want him back.

◇

I did not mean the kids when I said the chickens have come home to roost; I meant Lex and me. I do want him back. For ideological reasons, as we used to say. He had never fallen down drunk, and Cookie and he were the couple we should be.

I wish I could sue the therapy establishment and whoever is in charge of modern morality. So he drank? That was no reason to go discuss it with anyone but him. Maybe not even him. Look the other way or take a bat to him, and if he hit me back, not run to some battered-wives shelter and go on television. Even Deborah Alter is not around to hear my complaint. I hear she is the head of a clinic somewhere on the West Coast. Wouldn't you know it'd be the West Coast?

It is time to compromise. Discuss, talk over, reach a consensus—that would bring Lex round. He is so reasonable, so manipulable. I am sure that's what friends would say, but I am not discussing anything personally important anymore. The Supreme Court appointments, maybe. That is what we used to do, discuss endlessly, and he always said yes and we would have sex and he would go on to do what he wanted. The hell with it all;

now that I have sold a script no one can accuse me... who cares?

Anyway, Damon has already received acceptances from two East Coast colleges, but I know he wants to go to the West Coast. To get away from his parents? Or because out there there is more of a varied base for his multi-cultural beliefs. Also, I sometimes do not know if he wants to be a social worker or a novelist, or something worse, a rock and roll drummer. And Katrina—oh God, I will not go into that. Lex and I should be as one on this. That's what we should discuss. Should we be laissez faire, hands off, all that easygoing child-rearing orientation the Sixties taught us? Yes, indeed. I called him for the first time since the last time he skipped a rent check.

Before I dialed, I practiced my old voice, the one that was unquestionably mine before I started to worry about his drinking.

"I was thinking of you," he said in his insinuating tone, very special with him. He paused just a second, then added, "Pussy."

This was going to be easy. What a bore. But a necessary compromise on my part: that's maturity.

I told him about Damon.

"He's beautiful, right," he said. "Hamm, hamm." I swear his voice vibrated in the pauses.

It made me tingle. A surprise. "We ought to plan about him," I said, and I let a little excitement into my voice. Actually, I could not stop it.

"I took him to my monthly checkup visit at Rendezvous," he said. "He's beautiful."

"Rendezvous?" I said, and had to clear my throat to say it. "Where's that?"

"You don't know?" he said, genuinely puzzled. "The Hamiltons, the maze. We call it Rendezvous. I have to take you. The yews are five feet tall now."

"Already?"

His voice dropped into seduction. He said, "I enriched the beds with unicorn manure."

What an opening! I said to myself. Be brisk, however, but don't sound that way. The fact is, I felt giggly and nervous: I've never been good at calculation, and I hate seduction.

"You're still an imp," I said, one of the few things I never accused him of when I was in my accusing stage.

"I can come over now," he said.

I played it cool. "Ask Cookie," I said. "She might have some ideas of her own about Damon."

"She's in New York until tomorrow," Lex said. "That's why I'm free—there's a Lexington Avenue shop that's interested in her drawings."

I forgot to say that Cookie is something of an artist. That is how she and Dino met. Or was it?—her stuff is tasteful boutique art, whereas Dino is a naturalist given to looking close at the dark side of things. Cookie's look is more of a sleepy glimpse: at vegetables or old shoes, potatoes and weeds choking a perennial bed. The starkest she ever gets is mud clinging to onions and leeks in a harvesting basket. There is a large market for it in touristy towns; you find them in those sweet-smelling shops among English bath soaps and scents. When he became bitter, Dino called it "the new banality." Or if someone referred to it with approval or even neutrality, he would merely say, "Please."

"Well, come on over," I said, and quick put out liquor bottles and ice in the silver ice bucket his family gave us and we never used. While running around busily, I accused myself of planning to tank him up. Better than seduction, I replied. I took off my shoes and washed my face and looked in the mirror. I am twenty years older, but I didn't let it bother me. I looked down at my bare feet and hoped he still found that attractive, what the hell. I was not striking out for new territory nor entering a maze.

The thought stopped me. A new twist for the soap I worked for independently. Rich people with a maze. I stood in the living room and looked out the front window without looking, letting my mind roam. What about a maze on a rooftop penthouse? Or a parterre? No, a maze. A new side to the character of the Donald Trump character. A trysting place. Too costly a setting. It could be faked. Lex would be flattered if I asked for his advice. First, discuss Damon, then my soap-plot twist.

The sound of his jeep coming to a sudden noisy halt—his old way of parking—took me out of my trance. He jumped down to the ground. He was wearing baggily-cut trousers and a skin-tight T-shirt. He turned around and reached into the floor of his car. The pants fitted snuggly in the back seat, that round and full rump that once tensed so expressively when I caressed it. He headed towards the door, and I saw that his beard was streaked with gray now. All in all, better looking than in the old days. Even more macho.

I opened the door before he got to it: I didn't want to see if he would try it without by-your-leave or if he would knock and dutifully wait for it to be opened. He handed me the plain paper bag he had reached for in the car. I looked in it before either of us said a word. An old hand mirror in a silver frame. Art deco.

"Remember?" he said.

I did, but I shook my head to keep from looking into his eyes: let him woo me much more than that.

"Remember great grandmother Pennyfeather? She told you it would come down to you if you had a daughter?"

"Oh yes," I said, and stepped aside to let him in. "She's sweet."

"She died," he said.

"Oh, I forgot," I replied, and I have to admit that my voice fell not in mourning but in disappointment that this kind of family talk—which was what I had hoped for—would not lead him back to me. Or even to romance—my last resort. And if sex, then, was the only means of getting him under my roof, that would be a bore. I think I've said that before. Anyway, it was not what I wanted.

I saw him notice my feet. He looked up at me with the kind of glee I remembered well. He sidled as if to look at Grandma Pennyfeather's mirror with me, but with one arm he reached round and let his hand fall on the small of my back, then slide farther into the parting. Might as well give in. I took a deep breath and reached down and felt him. He picked me up without huffing—strong as ever—and carried me straight to the bedroom.

He checked the room with one glance and bounced me on the bed. “New sheets,” he said, then laughed when he found I was not wearing anything under my granny dress. “My girl,” he said, and went to work.

Again, I thought, what the hell. I've got him, that is the important thing. I had hardly finished the thought when I began trilling and thrashing, grabbing and pressing. That familiar flesh so comforting in the midst of shock and exhilaration. Slivers of memory, half idea, half feeling, found their way into the waves of emotion we rode, until I ceased to think at all.

When I came to, I was young again, young as before the children were born and Lex and I did not need beds or new sheets or even a roof to enjoy one another. On this note I slid off into dreamless sleep and floated slowly awake to find he had done the same. I was bathed in his perspiration. I had forgotten this about him. It is more pleasurable than it sounds. Clean perspiration: I was laved. His head on my breast. His black curly hair, without a single gray thread, was flattened round his forehead in ringlets, and I looked down at him and smiled to myself. He could not see me but he responded. He smiled without opening his eyes and took my nipple in his mouth. I was at peace. I guess that should be the end of this story, but it is not. Rejuvenation, what could be better or happier than that, right? Carefree, that's what being young means. And I had got him back. But I was to suffer a relapse.

In a moment, he nipped me, and I saw him squinch up his eyes in mock deep sleep.

I tapped him on the nose as in the old days.

He looked at me gleefully. "Don't you wish Cookie would stay in town?"

I chuckled.

"Huh, pussy?"

I thought about it.

I said, "Only a couple of times a month."

This time it was he who laughed. I had said it as a quip, but the idea took hold of me.

"Really?" he said, half-believing me now.

My reply in turn was half rebuke. "Let's talk about Damon's future."

He began to take liberties again. Leisurely, gently. Yes, I was able to say to myself this time round, for I was not at so high a pitch, this matinee is better than marriage and taking care of his smelly socks. We came out of it this second time with no need for sleep. A kind of relaxed self-assurance took the place of catharsis.

"What *are* we going to about Cookie?" he said in a while.

To the third or fourth variation of that question, I said, "Nothing."

"What!" he said.

"She's your wife," I said.

"But—"

"I'm not married," I said. "I'm available—now and then. But not for marriage."

I might have put it differently. I might have said, "I'm sorry, Lex, I made a mistake asking you over. Forgive and forget, okay?" But I did not.

He sat up. "And I was thinking we had made a garden today. A perennial center in a parterre."

He jumped out and headed for the kitchen to get a tall glass of iced water to replenish what he had lost. His buttocks were heftier, yes, and Cookie had, indeed, taught him a thing or two. As in the days when the kids slept soundly and he often walked around the house in that state, the tinkle of ice cubes announced his return.

I had learned a thing or two myself. I called to him before he reached the bedroom door, "Life is a maze—with no center, just these nice nooks and crannies. I don't want to go the center—or anything else."

He stood in the doorway and said, "But I could've sworn you wanted me back," he said.

I said, "I wanted to talk about Damon."

"I could've sworn," he repeated, and now stood naked by my bed. Not unhappy by the looks of him.

I said, "A lot you know about women," and grabbed his handle and pulled him into bed. What the hell, we could find some way to get rid of Cookie. Back to Dino? One thing though, no counselor this time.

What Hurts

From the days when she documented midtown for Loyalist Spain—and got chased by cops on horseback—to the present, marching in the Gay Pride parade with a sign declaring *I Am Proud Of My Gay Granddaughter*—Gladys never counted the cost of her political commitments. Dates forgotten in the excitement of joining a 1930's picket line that she happened upon, jobs lost, young men discouraged.

Her straight grandson, half-sitting on the window sill of her hospital room, said, "You could've married the head of Chase Manhattan? Oh, no!"

Her daughter, Rosa, came out of the room's toilet, which she had gone into to inspect, commented. "Daddy wasn't a bad catch. My daddy, that is. A partnership in a nice, old law firm."

Her son told himself this was not a rebuke.

What? What? Gladys thought.

Her gay granddaughter looked at Gladys with worshipful eyes. "You didn't even give it a thought, did you? You didn't care about Chase Manhattan, oh, wow!"

"I don't know..." Gladys said, as if it were a problem of focusing, as when she forgot to take her reading glasses to the A & P and could not consequently scan the containers for chemical ingredients or sugar and sodium. "I knew him, if that's what you mean."

"He wanted to know her, believe me—in a biblical sense," said Rosa who had, as Gladys would have put it, spilled the beans about Chase Manhattan.

Gladys made an attempt at pursuing her lips, but she was not good at that and so, as with all non-political issues, her disapproval evaporated.

"Grandma!" her gay granddaughter said. "I'm so proud of you."

Her grandson said, "This family is a matriarchy."

Her daughter, Rosa, laughed.

"Salacious remarks are always a diversionary tactic," Gladys recited. "I'm sorry," she added, but did not know why.

Her grandson said, "Matriarchies aren't that. What could be salacious about them?"

"What?" Gladys said, having already forgotten.

Rosa explained to her son. "She's complaining about what I said, not about you. I was named after Rosa Luxembourg, you know, and must act upright on all occasions. Whereas she marches with transvestites and whatnots."

"That's a strange statement," her daughter said.

Rosa raised the tote bag she carried. "In case you stay overnight," she explained to her mother. "Your own nightgown and slippers and stuff."

Gladys was trying to remember why next week was not a good time for the tests, but she smiled anyway. She was always automatically solicitous with her daughter—she had been apologizing to her, more or less, all her life.

"I won't be needing those things," she said when she caught up with what was being said. She reached out from her upright sitting position on the hospital bed and touched her arm. "I'm sorry, dear. Did I sound sharp?"

Gladys kept her eyes on Rosa although she was thinking of Rosa's husband. He had been a Marxist economist when they were young and now was a business consultant to big corporations. It was he whom she should be sharp with. Yes.

"It goes without saying..." Rosa began.

"Mother," her granddaughter said. "Please."

"Okay, okay," Rosa said. "Actually, I want to talk to your doctor. I've other things on my mind than your old beaux. Who is he? I've been meaning to ask."

Other things? Gladys thought. She must not respond. The nightgown and slippers were bad enough auguries. Dr. Nathan had also suggested she might have experienced a minor stroke, but she had not reported that: it signified little or nothing. She parted her lips, touched Rosa again, then changed her mind and shook her head. It stopped them.

"Where were we?" her grandson said. "This family's conversation is like riding the A train. You get bounced around, but you're hurtling to nowhere."

His sister said, "You must've prepared that line." She was immediately sorry. "I do it all the time, too, but then I forget all my witticisms when the time for them comes round."

"Well, actually, I thought of it on the A train," he said. "It was just after Thanksgiving and I was thinking about us and all."

"How nice," Gladys said, happy she had heard that: she loved her grandson and occasionally worried she might be unintentionally slighting him because he was apolitical.

"What were you doing on the A train?" his sister asked. "A new girlfriend?"

He said, "I wasn't going up there to buy drugs, I'll say that much."

Rosa said to Gladys, "You have very privileged grandchildren—they never go any farther uptown on the West Side than Lincoln Center or the Metropolitan on the East Side."

"Who goes to Lincoln Center?" her son said. "I was seeing a Latino friend home.

"If it comes to that..." Gladys said, and drifted off. It pained her to think of her own privileged beginnings in the city, her parents' townhouse in the Village, Grace Church Sunday mornings, the grand Sunday luncheons their cook prepared...

"Does it hurt, Grandma?" her granddaughter asked, looking at her gravely.

"What?" Gladys said. It was a Washington delegation she was committed to for next week. To lobby for a conservation law coming up. And for continuing the anti-apartheid boycott and, if there was time, against an anti-Cuba measure those dreadful exiles were sponsoring. "Oh, no, dear, it's just tests for tests' sakes. Biopsies, sonar something or the other. I've personally got no complaints."

It was a relief for the three of them that she was, finally, talking about it, but despite all the gambits they had thought of for the moment when the subject came up, they were unprepared for her off-center approach and said nothing.

"What hurts," she said, and she was no longer talking to her granddaughter alone, "what hurts is that people may think the good fight if over, that socialism is dead."

A keening silence hung in the still air of the room.

Then Gladys abruptly turned to her grandson, impatient that today she seemed to catch up so slowly with everything that was said. She asked, "A Dominican, sweetheart?"

He nodded. If his sister and mother were not there, he would have winked to let her know it was someone special. He did anyway, but, of course, Gladys did not notice.

Rosa asked no one in particular, "Did she say a Dominican sweetheart or a Dominican (pause) sweetheart?"

Her daughter said, "I knew it."

"I understand Washington Heights is," Gladys began but did not get to finish her question. "That is it—"

Rosa said, "Mostly Dominican."

"Yes," her son said. "Definitely."

Gladys said, "I daresay they remember President Johnson's dastardly invasion... Whatever happened?..." She tried to recall the activities of the ad hoc committee they had formed to call a press conference.

Rosa said, "It got wiped off the agenda by Viet Nam."

"My friend never mentioned it," her son said. He looked at his grandmother. "There was an invasion?"

But that was only yesterday, Gladys thought.

He added, "I'll ask her."

Rosa said, "She must be a bimbo not to know."

Her daughter said, "Mother, that's sexist."

"I know it is," Rosa said. "But for a Dominican not to know about Bosch and the invasion—"

"Bosch, that was his name," Gladys said. "He was only mildly liberal."

Rosa continued, "It would be like your not having heard about the Kennedy assassination."

Her son laughed. "We just didn't happen to talk about it. Well, *I* didn't know—so why should she make it an issue when we've only just met? Right?"

His sister said, "You didn't know about the Kennedy assassination?"

"Of course, I know about the Kennedy assassinations," he said. "Mom exaggerates."

"To make a point," Rosa explained.

"We know too much about Jack Kennedy's assassination," he said. "Too much."

"Well, dear, I don't know about that," Gladys said. They turned to her respectfully although they knew what she was going to say. "I don't think we know enough about its real aims—that it was meant to spur us on to try once more to get rid of Fidel by framing Oswald as a Communist agent, but the Cubans were too smart to let them get away with that. It wouldn't wash. I think I may have told you about this and the French journalist who happened to be with Fidel when the news came?…"

"Oh, yes, Grandma," he said, with a chuckle that took the sting out of his reply. "You certainly have told us."

"And others," Rosa said.

"I believe you, Grandma," her granddaughter said eagerly. "I mean, I want to hear it."

"In political matters you have to keep repeating ideas and programs over and over again," Gladys said, "in order for them to get a hearing. Winning converts for one's programs requires it—it's not like…not like—"

Rosa said, "Real life," with assurance, and began to laugh in expectation that the others would join her.

There was a pause.

Her daughter said, "It is real life to insist, to insist passionately. People have been rushing into the streets throughout modern history, insisting…"

"That's like Gertrude Stein," her brother said. "I think I'm becoming literary. But isn't writing going out of fashion?"

His mother said, "I thought you've been using a lot more similes and metaphors than you used to."

Gladys said, "That's very nice… All writers want to change the world. You will, too." She looked at him contemplatively. "What was it Stein said?"

After a pause, he said, "Oh, I forgot about that, Grandma, didn't I? It's insistence not repetition, she said, I am insisting not repeating. Get it?"

"Really?" said Rosa.

He turned to his sister. "She was a little goofy, but she was very interesting, you know."

She waved a hand. "You can also talk to me about straight authors, you know."

Gladys sighed. "She didn't like Hemingway being to involved with Loyalist Spain."

Her granddaughter moaned. "Those apolitical old dykes. They figured, don't rock the boat too much. Chop down trees, climb mountains, shoot the rapids—show them you're healthy, ho-ho."

Rosa said, "That's hardly what she and Toklas did."

"I like the way she comes at a story," her son said. "Roundabout. Never on the nose."

Gladys said, "You don't prefer a writer to come right out and say what he means?"

Her granddaughter said, "Or *she* means."

Rosa laughed.

"Mother," the girl said, and let her reprimand peter out. Instead, she smiled at Gladys.

Her brother spoke to his grandmother, as if over the heads of his sister and mother. "Well, you know, in literature the object is not to impart—"

His mother said, "Your grandmother is very well read. Better than most."

"Yes," her daughter said, in uneasy agreement.

"What were you going to say?" his grandmother asked him. "Dear?"

"Nothing important," he said.

Gladys reminded him. "In literature..."

He smiled at her and said nothing.

Rosa asked, "Did Dr. Nathan say when he'll..."

No one approved of her question.

In a moment, Gladys said, "Remind me when he comes to ask him if he is related to the Dr. Nathan who was Einstein's good friend. Dr. Nathan was always available for every good cause."

Rosa said, "There are other things I want to ask him about."

Gladys continued, "I served under him in many a committee for years. Then I made the board of a Spanish Republican committee that once had to meet at his apartment. For me it was like graduating. There was a little grandson there..."

Rosa said, "Let's not go into that with him today."

"He won't have any new information," Gladys said. "He has already told me they expect it's cancer. He and I will just discuss the dates for tests—"

"He and I will discuss other things," Rosa said. "I want to ask him about oncologists. Is he bringing one in and who? I don't suppose you asked him. We have to have a second opinion, maybe a third."

"Dear, the whole thing's routine now," Gladys said. "All that is old stuff and they must have a course they follow with everyone—" she let her voice rise to announce she was being light-hearted—"regardless of race, color or creed."

"Gladys," Rosa warned her by addressing her familiarly.

"Remind me, too," Gladys added, "to make sure he understands that he can't schedule me for Tuesday, Wednesday or Thursday."

"Why?" Rosa said, and immediately felt she had been sidetracked about all the things she wanted to discuss with the doctor. As a result she repeated more emphatically, "Why?"

"I'm on a Washington delegation," Gladys said.

"You are not going, Gladys," Rosa said. "You may not cross me on this."

"It's not simply about the conservation measure coming up, there is also a danger," her mother said, "that this awful administration will lift the sanctions on the South Africans before apartheid is fully overthrown."

Rosa said, "There is always a danger."

"There are people who must be reached," Gladys said. "No one's indispensable, but there are people who will see me. They'll at least have to listen."

"Good, Grandma, put the screws on them," her granddaughter said. "Out them."

"Nonsense," Rosa said. "You're going to rest and get your tests. I'll stay in the city with you."

Gladys listened to her as if biding her time.

"I'm not a politician you mean to have your way with, Gladys," Rosa said. "I didn't come down from Connecticut to fall in with your madness."

Madness? Gladys sat up straighter. "Why are you so upset?" she asked. "I told you it's nothing." She forced a chuckle. "Besides, on apartheid it's your senator I want to see. We went to the same schools in New York from kindergarten on, until prep school."

Rosa spoke to her children. "I'm going to need your support. You speak to her; I'll speak to the doctor."

Gladys reached out a hand to Rosa again, meaning many things by the gesture. "Dear, why don't you come with me to Washington. You'll meet Bootsy and that will carry weight—you're actually a constituent. It will be fun."

Rosa said, "Oh, sure."

"Remember the old days, dear?' her mother said. "I used to take you with me everywhere."

Her grandson said, "Like the Latinos, they take their kids along all the time, no matter how late."

His sister said, "They're right, they know how to live—instinctively."

Rosa glared at her. "My outings were a pretty steady diet of political demonstrations," Rosa said. She hiccuped. Before she could get a hand up to her mouth, it turned into a sob. She was stunned.

So were the others.

"God damn it," Rosa said, mostly to herself.

The others were now embarrassed as well. Gladys smoothed the top sheet of her bed. Her granddaughter got up, looked about and started towards her grandmother and then returned to her chair. Her brother shifted his position and looked out the window.

When he turned around, he looked past his mother towards the corridor and this alerted Gladys. She half-turned and graciously lifted a hand at the man in the white smock who stood in the doorway. "Dr. Nathan," she said. "You came just as you said."

He smiled, nodded, walked into the room, and briefly glanced at the others.

"I don't think you've met my daughter," Gladys said, and indicated her. "And these are my grandchildren."

He smiled and nodded again. To Rosa, he said, "I'm glad you're here."

Rosa's daughter said, "I'm not leaving," as if to make up for her uncertain movements a moment earlier.

Rosa said, "Doctor, I would have come with her, but she didn't let anyone know, just my answering machine."

Dr. Nathan was young. He held up both hands and looked at Gladys' granddaughter a second time. "Don't anyone move. The fact is, there is nothing more to say than what I've said before."

He once more looked from one to the other. "Has Mrs. Mayhew told you it could be cancer?'

Everyone nodded.

Rosa said, "I want to talk to you about that."

"Anytime," Dr. Nathan said, "but after we have done a few more tests." He turned to Gladys. "I'm keeping you here overnight, for the minor ones. Blood tests, urine, x-rays—you'll leave, say, by noon tomorrow. At the latest three."

Rosa held up the tote bag.

"Round one," her son said.

Dr. Nathan lifted his eyebrows quizzically.

The granddaughter said, "Grandma was not expecting that."

Dr. Nathan continued, "But next week I want you in for extensive ones. I've talked to colleagues—"

Gladys said, "I think you said I could be away Tuesday, Wednesday and Thursday. I need to; it should be no trouble, right?"

Dr. Nathan looked down, not wishing to contradict her: it had never come up. "I don't want to put it off any further than that—especially if the bleeding gets worse before then."

Rosa said, "There's no need to put it off, doctor."

"No, just for those few days," Gladys said. "Good, it's all settled."

"Doctor?" Rosa said.

Gladys hurried to explain before he mentioned the stroke. "My daughter will be with me next week."

"So will I," said her granddaughter.

"If Dr. Nathan says yes," her grandson said, "I'm going to Washington, too."

"Washington?" Dr. Nathan asked, and looked at Gladys, and when she nodded, paused and nodded, too. "Okay, but nothing strenuous," he said. "I expect you first thing Friday morning of next week. And tomorrow morning I may pass by and look in on you."

"I want to see you," Rosa said.

"I remember," Dr. Nathan said.

"Dr. Nathan, a personal question," Gladys said in a change of tone. "I've been meaning to ask you since Dr. Strahan sent me to you."

"Yes," he said, hoping to take the conversation away from his patient's daughter: she was anxious and this distraction might help.

"Are you, by chance, related to another Dr. Nathan I once knew—Dr. Otto Nathan?" she asked.

"Otto?" he said. "What was his field?"

It occurred to her that she did not know. His field was the world, but it might not seem polite to say so.

She saw the looks on her grandchildren's faces—genuinely sympathetic to her disappointment—and did not allow herself to conclude that there was a premonition of death in all this real hurt. She must put it aside, as he had so many defeats, and take action. She quickly began to tell the young doctor about dear Otto Nathan. That was the only action she could think of, for now. Someone else would know about him.

An Idea for a Story

The summer was coming to an end. This was the third party of the week: Lizzie's big bash. I stood at her patio's railing. Long, broad lawns opened wondrously ahead. At the other parties they sloped down to variable Maine waters. Not at Lizzie's; she summered in town, at an elegant seaside one. She conformed, but always with a demur, restless as a teen-age girl trying out variations of her name. She was not a girl any longer and I was not a boy, but we both knew, I believe, about the longings of youth that still hang on late in life. Like being at this greensward in Maine. Perhaps, like the good hostess she was, she would come look at it with me.

The salt in the air heightened the exhilarating smell of the pines. You knew where you were despite the enclosure of the grounds by a stand of firs. Lizzie must have wanted this effect, oh, yes. She insisted on her presence as much as the sea did. She must be sixty-five; I never meant to give a woman a decade older than I this much thought. Only enough to get on her guest list—here and in Boston and London. And here I was; no need of more from her. I was pleased with myself and my thoughts. I always know where I am. I am a writer: I store away unannounced thoughts and not to know where I am gives me vertigo.

I looked at the pines and felt again—more tranquilly, of course—the emotion that had made me exclaim at yesterday's party. Strictly a middle-class affair, that one, though more upper than lower. The party began with drinks at the yacht club and we were all boated from there to the island at the cove's mouth for the picnic. Two amiable retired businessmen, buoyed by comfortable inheritances and dutifully earned stock options, were walking with me from the veranda to the pier. In the water were boats, each with its dinghy, and on the pier women in colored dresses. With the sun in my eyes the scene beyond glittered almost painfully. I asked myself: How did I get here? And on the sort of impulse I don't usually indulge I said to my companions, "Look at the magnificent panorama—it's like *The Beach At Deauville*! What is a cigarmaker's son from Tampa, Florida doing here?"

There is a story in this, I immediately thought. A ready made title, too.

They were embarrassed. "Not at all," one said inconsequentially, and the other gurgled his response. Of course, they didn't know what to say. They were not Lizzie's intellectuals who have laughed and, of course, not replied. Nor were they Bostonians, like the other regulars at Lizzie's parties. Bostonians of old families, that is—prepared by history for any social untowardness. A Bostonian who did not know the impressionist canon would have immediately announced it and made one feel pretentious. But not these contented men, kindly in retirement; they were embarrassed now and later would somehow be pleased.

Was there a story in all this? Indeed, how did I get here? *The Beach At Deauville*. The first time I walked into the impressionist rooms at the Met I felt I had just stopped running and was breathing in spurts of ecstacy. I was seventeen and worked as a busboy. Yes, I must write that story.

I turned slightly at the patio railing to check, as if the notion that there might be a story in this Maine summering of mine required it, that Lizzie's perfect Georgian house was paradigmatically there. Every spring she had its lemony-yellow color refreshed with a coat of paint. She was not due to arrive with her husband until much later, but the house, like a proper young girl, stood there in all its pristine beauty at the head of Main Street to greet the summer people who arrived at the beginning of June. Lizzie had bought and refurbished it with the royalties of her one novel, inexplicably a best-seller, then a Broadway musical, and finally a movie. That she had not inherited the house seemed to me the only cachet that life had withheld from her. This was only the second summer I visited it. That was one of many things life had withheld from me, a son of cigar makers.

I thought: It's time I slept with Lizzie. That would surely make a good story. Changed, of course; move the scene away from Maine to the Cape or the Hamptons. No, that would coarsen Lizzie's social tone. The Cape was fine for the forties, when she was still young and getting in touch with her Boston heritage. But the Hamptons, never.

Behind me were other guests at glass-topped white tables, all of them remarkably proper for the acerb Trotskyite Lizzie had been in the thirties. At one sat Nagel, the art historian, whom I left a moment ago when he mentioned for the second time that he had turned down the curatorship of a Texas oilman's museum; now I wanted to ask him about *The Beach At Deauville.* At another were my wife and Lizzie's current husband, both proper enough to be guests and no more. I'm leaving them out of this; neither belongs in the foreground of any story.

Lizzie was still as acerb as ever—a brilliant social critic, even her wounded critics conceded—but her radicalism showed itself mostly in an amused, affectionate attitude towards Trotskyite activists in the Third World. In any case, her Boston forefathers (she was born in Iowa) reemerged in the correctness of her parties—no paper plates or plastic cups or food prepared anywhere but her own kitchen; and in the heterodoxy of her guests—Republicans and writers and Indian students today. Her intellectual adventuresomeness—and theirs—could be said to be evidenced in the elegant amalgam of her New England house—painted floors, English chintzes, French country furniture, Morris wallpaper, abstract expressionist paintings.

Would she have excluded Edgar Allan Poe? Only if he were a Stalinist. Had she read my autobiographical novel? Did she know about my family's Communist past? Best leave that out of the story—too complex.

Lizzie's books were like her guests, proper but a strange mix. Her novel was not the first of her books; that was a journalistic group picture of the Brain Trust, which snubbed them and also FDR; another book destroyed whatever audience was left for H. G. Wells and the dishwater realists; an appreciative survey of the German expressionists boosted the prices of Egon Schieles in the United States and, since it was 1950, titillated readers with its cool discussion of eroticism in family life; and, of course, the book on the Kennedys that kept many persons away from ceremonies at the various Kennedy memorials for fear of being considered both intellectually and morally second-rate.

Second-rate. Could there be a worse fate in Lizzie's crowd?

The poet Toms (wonderful old Boston name; you couldn't appropriate it for a story—he had made it so known—no more than you would call any fictional protagonist Pound) burst out of the house, a beautiful faience plate in one hand, a cigarette and drink in the other, and headed for me, determinedly. Even an old fire chief of a Boston lady who would have easily intimidated me could not stop him. "Toms, boy, pick up my napkin," she said, and he only nodded and kept going with his wild look. His walk was something of a long hard dash; he had been skulking behind doors. It was his first week back in the States after two years in Devon with an earl's widow, and he had come first to the Toms' summer cottage nearby. In a week he would be in New York, and if by then the newspapers had not announced the end of that affair, a poem of his in the New York Review of Books would.

He stared at me with his wild man's look, ran a hand through his hair, and asked me in a sweet, seductive voice, "Do you go to Cuba anymore?"

"Remember, I asked you when we first met..." And he paused slightly, the kind of breath of a pause signalled in his early poems by a virgule; he had picked it up from William Carlos Williams (in the days when he, Toms, converted to Catholicism and developed stigmata with each of his manic lows) and made it so popular that the Beats began to use slant signs more often than words. He dropped the virgule then. *Let me bequeath the virgule ere I go*, he wrote in a strict sonnet, likening the iambic pentameter to the discipline of life and dogma.

That pause, it let me know various things. One of them, that he believed I had solaced his wife while he was in England. I continued smiling.

He spoke on the next beat. "I did, didn't I; I asked you if the Cubans would permit publication of Yeats' conservative poems? And you said no."

Oblique castigation?

I said, "I said yes if it were Yeats, no if it were a live Cuban poet as desirous of speaking for Cuba as Yeats was for—"

Toms interrupted. "For the world, chaps, for the whole world. That's for whom the old man spoke." And he stared down into Lizzie's grass and contemplated his own hubris. "Him and his fairies at the bottom of his garden." He forgot all about castigating me and laughed and jiggled the ice in his empty drink for reverberating clamor.

"It's a beautiful day," I said.

"I'm not going to grow old," he said. "I'd rather run after boys than write landscape poetry."

"Were you thinking of Yeats?"

"God, no, Wordsworth."

"And I'm not going to visit Cuba anymore."

"I'm sorry about that. You used to talk about Cuba as if she were a woman." He gave a mad laugh and waved away his old wife, Betty, who stuck to him as to a roller coaster and tried to approach us now. He prodded by elbow with the cheerful rim of his Mustier plate, into which he had piled Lizzie's superb cold-rice salad and the lemon-oregano chicken and a ragged piece of baguette with brie. Betty retreated. "Ha-ha, maybe that's what drew you there. Wallace Stevens used to talk about those Cuban *mulatas*. And you Latins aren't New Englanders—you act on your autoerotic images."

"Celt, that's what I am."

"Oh, you're going to pretend an interest in baseball next, like all the fake intellectuals. In England no one talks cricket."

"No, the real Celtics. All my family are Galicians. Not Cubans. The northwest of Spain. From there the Celts invaded Ireland."

"Yeats' Ireland?"

"The very one."

"Oh," he said. He stuck a couple of fingers in his plate. "There's a bit of bloody lobster in this rice—and it's cold. Lizzie's become pretentious, bringing a Basque cook to a Maine town. Why can't she serve a casserole like everyone else?"

"Lizzie herself—"

"Lizzie could cook once and do other things, too—" He broke off and laughed his mad laugh and slowly leaned over the patio railing and let his plate float down to the grass.

Betty showed up immediately. She picked up the plate and gathered up a chicken breast and returned it to the plate.

"Leave the rice—it's good for the lawn, turns into compost," Toms said, and turned away from her. He shook his head at me conspiratorially—we had both known Betty, hadn't we?

Poor Betty, she must be back to tracking him wherever he went: calling friends to tell them Toms was on his way to them, asking them to call her when he left. Betty had published a book of short stories, and Lizzie once joked that life with Toms only left her time for short fiction.

As soon as Betty was out of hearing, I said, "I took Betty to one of those PEN things where only young people on the make go."

"And the two of you had no stomach for anything later but for a bar—who cares what you did!"

"Well, I did go to a bar—alone."

"Guilt drove you to it."

"There was no reason for guilt, damn it."

"Aha!"

"I'll tell you where I went. The old Cedar Bar expecting there'd be no one there. I ordered a beer, and there was de Kooning. The first time since the sixties, he said."

Toms laughed. I laughed. I suddenly felt I didn't have to write a story about my worrisome past. Toms, the day; it was all fine.

But then the old fire chief got up from her white garden seat and headed for us after veering to windward and picking up Lizzie who humored her as she wouldn't any literary person. Lizzie was very kind to old Boston.

Toms said, "Oh, damn," but he was more old Boston than either of them, and, anyway, it was me the old woman headed for. She looked me over like a Marine inspection sergeant. "Lizzie, who is this man? He doesn't look like one of your husband's government friends—nor like a disreputable writer."

"My dear," said Lizzie. "Surely there are more categories than that."

"Well, he doesn't look like a stuffy professor."

Toms said, "You know, he says he Celtic."

"I didn't know," Lizzie said with a certain hauteur, and introduced me.

The old lady looked right into my eyes and said, "There was Fenollosa and later Santayana, but your—"

"When Boston was Boston, people would have known his name," Lizzie said, and neither she nor the old fire chief heard Toms say, "I don't know if that's a compliment," as Lizzie led her away. Lizzie still walked like a young girl.

She was back in a moment. She held her shoulders back and her chin up as when engaged on an expedition of some moment. To Toms she said: "I expect you to save the French reading circle from that old bore and Victor Hugo." To me: "I do not believe that you're not fluent in French."

Toms glowered. "I suppose you want St. John Perse."

"No, Claudel." She turned to me. "Shouldn't we be reading Claudel?"

"Someone delicate, of course," Toms said, and held on to his scowling grimace.

"Oh, I pardon Paul Claudel," I said. "Pardon him for writing well."

Lizzie patted the back of my hand to signify I need not have, in *their* company, paraphrased more than the first line. I trapped her hand in mine.

Toms said, "Latins suffer no guilt, no guilt whatever." I would not drop Lizzie's hand no matter how much he stared. "They foist those populist dictators on us, tumble our wives, corrupt our taste with old librarians like Borges..."

Lizzie laughed her wonderful deep laugh.

I made my mistake. "I read somewhere a comment of Moravia's," I said. "He said, 'Once I used to feel so unhappy, so hopeless that I wandered the streets in despair, so doomed that I thought often of stepping into traffic and being done with it. That was in the afternoons, of course—in the mornings I wrote.'"

Lizzie took her hand away. She needed it to exclaim, "Where does that leave *me*!" And she walked away.

"That's a damnable thing," Toms said. "Cynical."

"Isn't there at least a touch of professionalism in all of us?" I said.

"Not me, not me," Toms said, looking about him. "Where the hell is that chicken?"

"You threw it away," I said. Damn that Lizzie, thinks she can have it both ways. You can't throw a party like this... There was a snub in her reply—had she implied I was a huckster?—and she'd tumble to me for it.

"You know damn well that you quoted Moravia for my edification and that Lizzie can't stand semi-Stalinists like him," Toms said, and quite unconsciously took a dueling stance. "I'm not a Catholic anymore, you know, I'm no easy mark for a literary gangster."

I did not hit him as I had been known to do when I played in the streets and on occasion was insulted by one of the other kids. "You want me to go get you another piece of chicken, you old drunk?" I said.

"Yes," he said softly, and looked at me from under his brows. "And I want you to know my despair is real. I can't walk through that crowd Lizzie invites—"

"You can't walk a straight line," I said, and we forgave one another.

"Hurry back with the chicken; I have to talk to you," he said, then reached out and grabbed my shoulder. "No, stay. One can't talk to other literary gents about what ails you and me."

"What ails *me*?"

"Come on, none of that aunty manner. I don't remember you going in for Jamesian locutions and discriminations. You and I, we've got that terrible yearning. I used to think time would cure the itch. But time has come and gone. It's not an itch either; it's not priapic. Why are women so important?"

"Very likely because they *are* important."

"No, no, their praise, not themselves."

"I make no such distinctions," I said, lying. "Tell no one, but they are our real souls. They hold the key that opens us up to civilization."

"Oh, I forgot you're Spanish. Idealize them and seduce them. No, traduce them. Go get my chicken. I thought I could talk to you. You're not an aunty, but you've got that overlay of Castilian manners. I thought you were real."

"You thought I was no gentleman. Tell the truth, you Wasp," I said. "I'll go get you your chicken."

"Yes, I'm probably just hungry," Toms said. "I had a camp counselor like you. I loved him. He was Irish and full of joy."

"Celtic."

"I went to talk to him once—I was going to confide in him, declare my love probably—and he said he'd noticed I had not eaten much of my dinner but that he'd sneak into the kitchen and get some food. He was right." Toms heaved a huge sigh. "I was ten."

"Do I get you your chicken?"

"You're a working-class fellow, aren't you?"

"How nice to hear the phrase," I said, and took a deep breath myself.

"What phrase?"

"I guess it's a compound adjective rather. Not a phrase, properly speaking—working-class hyphenated, that is."

"I'm going to have to be hospitalized again," Toms said, again with a wild look. "I've been away two years and all that anyone is embattled about is correct usage.

There's not a vestige of ideology left in our crowd, in our country. What's happened!"

"*I*'m enjoying myself," I said. "In fact, I was thinking of my working-class origins."

How did I get here? That's what I must write about. What would my sweet old anarcho-syndicalist grandfather have said?

"I used the phrase *in fact* the other day—or was it earlier today?—and Lizzie told me I meant indeed not in fact and sent me back to Fowler."

"And did you go?"

"What's the matter with you? Let Fowler come to me! Even Betty—who was not too bright when she was my student at Smith—even she gave me a little lecture on should and would. I said to her, I should prefer it if you were speaking of obligations and desires and not of grammatical housekeeping, and she hadn't the wit to laugh."

"Perhaps she was speaking of such matters in her way."

"Perhaps." He lit a cigarette with the butt of the one he had been chewing at the corner of his mouth. "I pushed her back on the bed immediately after and covered her and that seemed to satisfy her in that superficial eighteenth-century way."

I laughed at the eighteenth-century characterization, but such confidences are, I believe, in fact and in deed boring. I said, "Perhaps grammatical concerns are an unconscious expression—"

"Cut it out," Toms said. "I prefer Marxist jargon to Freudian—oh, God, how pretentious we could sound at Partisan Review, remember? But you..."

"I couldn't afford to write for Partisan Review," I said. "I still can't."

"What about those best-sellers? But let's not talk about that; it's not good for me," Toms said. "They're all dying out, those old Trotskyites, or writing their memoirs."

He lifted an arm and threw his glass towards the firs, but, of course, it fell far short of them. He was no left fielder cutting a runner off at home base; he was just a poet. But there was always Betty—she streaked past us for the glass. It was probably good Baccarat. Toms didn't glance at her; he let himself down slowly and sat at the patio's edge.

I did not look back at the others sitting at the tables and engaging in light talk, as one should at a garden party, but surely this gesturing of Toms' would be talked about later. Could I use it in my story? Did it signify the aristocracy was, unlike the state, withering away? Deteriorating? That Lizzie was Madame Verdurin in her last guise as the Princess des Guermantes?

Should I squat with Toms? I wore a silk and linen white suit and had to be careful. I should leave him: I was no Mailer and could not use him as material until he died. Too obvious. And by the time he died his case wouldn't be up-to-date and significant. That's what I wrote—up-to-date stories, but none that cannibalized people I knew. Bad manners, that. No Spaniard would do it; I could at least be true to that past.

I changed my mind, suddenly, right there, as Betty hurried across the acres of lawn. I'd write about them all. I said, "I'm feeling the way you did when you wrote *After Words*."

"God, how was that!"

"Traitorous," I said.

"Traitorous?" Toms repeated. "Too strong. You should remember what that bastard Rahv said about my Catholicism—*Tums*, he called it, a mild antidote for Wasp dyspepsia." Toms laughed. "Not bad, that's why I remember it."

The story I would write could be less about Lizzie and the itch than about incommunicability among the communicators. No, it must be about selling out. That was my mood these days. Incommunicability was a glut on the market.

"Anyway, it's impossible to be treasonous in America," Toms said. "You can't really trash our country."

Ah, it was good to hear him say our country, emphasis on the plural adjectival pronoun. In, out, patriotically I was always a revolving door.

"Not the way Shaw did," he was saying when I came to, "so that people—especially people who are our targets—feel insulted. It's maddening."

"All right, but I *can* say that lately I've been feeling that I've sold out," I said, and felt for an instant—that was all the time Toms allowed me—the thrill of confession to a peer.

Toms cut me off with a stare in which I could see those Danas and Phillipses and Wentworths whom he had let us know in his poetry he was descended from—

they were all judging me. Who was I to think I had some birthright to sell out?

"Are you going to write a movie script?" he said finally. "That's what selling out meant once. Does it mean anything now? Does it even apply? Let's get another drink."

I laughed. Obviously I couldn't act out my idea for a story with him. Life was more intractable than prose.

"Oh, I know what you mean. I should be an authority on guilt and treason," he said, and muttered, "Good Betty," as she went by looking scared by what the thrown glass might portend. "You mean my guilt at having offended the Protestantism that all my ancestors—puritans and royalists, abolitionists and conservatives—held in common. You suffering from guilt, big boy?"

"I'll get us both a drink," I said, keeping any further confessions for my story.

"Come here, you Latin satyr," he said, and reached up and grabbed my trousers and held on.

I stopped. I didn't think my trousers could slide off that easily, but I thought, How would this work in my story, and that stopped me. To be standing on this fashionable lawn suddenly down to my Dior bikini shorts? Ideology as farce—did I want that?

Lizzie appeared at our side. "Tommy," she said, articulating even more clearly than usual, "your Betty is in a fright that you're getting soused. Are you getting soused?"

Something had to happen in my story. You can't just place a lugubrious hero on a lawn and expect people to read on. I should look to frightened Betty for a lifelike surprise, except that the real Betty never would burst into life; that impulse had long ago been suppressed in her.

My wife? No, she's out of this story.

"He's all right," I said to Lizzie. "But if he doesn't let go soon I shall be standing here in my underwear."

Let the impulse come from me.

So I said to Lizzie, "Would you like that?"

She knew what that meant: she had been wooed a lot. Just as she had articulated more clearly for Toms, she held her head more aloofly than usual in turning to me. Distancing was something one had to master among Wasps.

"Would that be nice?" she said, then smiled her famous smile. It made everything charming and acceptable, but the position of her head had not changed. "Shall I give Tommy the go ahead?"

Toms wasn't listening, though his hand hung on like a child's.

I said in as low a voice as I could register, "Let's try it, Lizzie."

"I'm a good girl, I am," Lizzie said, and shook her head so that her hair flew to the sides, like the actress who in our generation had played Liza.

"Lizzie," I said, and allowed my voice to shake with desire. "Lizzie."

Her face looked at me with eyes opened wide. It shone intensely; it was like a close-up on a TV screen. Had we not been standing there as on a huge life screen for all the party to see, I should have extended a hand

and grabbed some intimate part of her, for it's the vulgar pull of flesh women succumb to. Only in stories—mine?—are seductions refined.

I lifted a hand. Did I dare?

"Yes?" she said sharply, and I recognized the close-up for what it was: another social observer observing. She might accept my advance and then again she might not. But for now a warning. Toms would be forgiven anything; I would not.

I felt an inspired rebuff. Lizzie had rejected the man I had placed on view, but not she alone: I participated in the expulsion. The blow was doubly hard. The blood seemed to leave my head. Between us we had created a third person, the man who was insulted and repelled, the cigarmaker's son, the genuine one in my story who no longer existed. I belonged here on this patio; I as not the child of my ancestors.

This was not the tone I wanted for my story. I wanted to call it *The Beach At Deauville* and let its scene be all sunlight and temptation, a radiant explanation for seduction and treason.

Toms saved me from vertigo. He let go his hand. "Go get us the drink," he said, and I was able to leave Lizzie hanging, to distance myself as coolly as she.

I could thus also check with Nagel, the art historian. I tapped him lightly on the shoulder and asked him with no explanation to describe for me the canvas of *The Beach At Deauville*.

He replied in the fruity voice academics fall into when asked a question they can answer expansively.

"The sea at the top of the canvas. In the foreground a very proper bourgeois scene. Couples dressed to the nines; they could be sitting in a cluttered Victorian drawing room. They're French, so they're even stiffer. And beyond them the sea, tamed."

"Not joyful?"

"Somber is the word you might use," Nagel said, and emitted a little chuckle announcing irony. "Only, that is, if you want to mix art and purely subjective emotions."

"I always do," I said. "I'm a barbarian."

None of this would do for my story. At the next table was my wife still talking to Lizzie's husband undisturbed. I must find another metaphor for my story.